# Wolves Will Be Wolves

## JD Nelson

GETTING HER BACK ............................................................1

I MUST PROTECT HER ........................................................25

A NEW HOME ....................................................................35

AT WIT'S END ...................................................................48

ANOTHER DAY, ANOTHER CONSORT ..............................51

PACK MENTALITY … OR JUST MENTAL ...........................59

A TRULY EPIC PACK MEETING .......................................66

AN UNEXPECTED HOUSEGUEST .....................................98

LUPINE AND FELINE BEHAVIOR ...................................114

MAKING A MAN OUT OF A CAT ...................................127

A HOMECOMING OF SORTS ..........................................139

EVERY DOG HAS ITS DAY .............................................146

HELPING YOUR MATE'S HUSBAND 101 .........................159

THE MAKING OF A NEW BREED ....................................174

*To Nels, always Nels*

# GETTING HER BACK

## OSWIN

Law Offices of Solon Manetas
Meadowbrook, Alabama
Petition No. 0120386

Date of Petition:  March 10

Full Name:  Oswin Morris

Mailing Address: PO Box 93720100

City: Thomasville    State: Alabama    Zip Code: 36784

Physical Address:  1351 Barnett St.

City: Thomasville    State: Alabama    Zip Code: 36784

Home Phone: 555-0177

Mobile Phone: 555-0136

E-Mail Address: OswinMorris@gmail.com

Marital Status: Mated

Spouse's Name:  Korrina Manetas Raines

Petition Details:  Oswin Morris, Alpha of the Thomasville wolf pack, petitions the court to force his mate, Korrina Manetas Raines, to return to the pack-lands to lead, as outlined in Werewolf Customs and Laws, 5th Edition, page 239, article 39104, section B.

I was pretty sure my beta delighted in my torment.

1

He was laughing at me in that special way he knew made my hackles rise … again. The same laugh he knew made me clench my teeth together and count down from ten to keep my hands from closing around his neck.

Aw, hell. Maybe I deserved it. I was acting like the biggest dick on the planet. Sadly, that was nothing new for me.

I mean, after all, it wasn't Klive's fault I was agitated. He was just being his usual slightly irritating but strangely endearing self. And he certainly wasn't the reason I was only a heartbeat away from wolfing out and pulling a move that hadn't been made since seventeen thirty-six. No, that honor belonged to my mate, Korrina. Beautiful, mysterious, infuriating Korrina.

Klive glanced over at me, sobering a bit before looking back at the road. "Listen, Oswin, I may be young, but even I can see that you're doing the right thing by the pack. We need an Alpha female to make it whole."

What he really meant was that I needed an Alpha female to make me whole. As usual, he was right. I wore my despair like a favorite tie. Even if they weren't supernatural, everyone in the pack would still be hyper-aware of the keening sense of loss my wolf felt. I needed Korrina, needed her in the most primal and basic of ways. I couldn't hide it.

"Plus," he added. "If you get any grouchier, we're going to have to get you a garbage can to live in."

I sighed. "I know you're right, but like this? She's going to rip my fucking throat out for forcing her hand."

Klive smirked but didn't look away from the road. "Maybe. Probably. There's only one way to find out."

I leaned back onto the headrest and stared up at the heavens. There was no probably about it. Korrina hadn't seen hide nor hair of me for three long years. And we didn't exactly leave each other on amicable terms.

I reached up to trace my finger across the faint scar on my jugular. She'd given it to me the last time we'd seen each other. I'd deserved it. I'd deserved it and a whole lot more. What I did to her was unforgivable.

"Last chance to turn around," Klive drawled. There was a hint of humor in his voice.

"No, I'm doing it. I have to," I said firmly, more to myself than him. "It's now or never."

"Never's not an option," he reminded me. "Never's a really long time for a werewolf."

I took a deep breath to steady myself and let it out slowly. "That's why we're here, kid."

Solon Manetas chose an isolated part of Meadowbrook for his law office. It was tucked away from the main road, down what must be the most depressing but eerily scenic gravel road in America. Draped to near darkness with the ancient vines of several thousand wisteria plants, the day turned to night the second we turned onto it. While wisteria wasn't uncommon in these parts, especially for a nymph settlement, I had to wonder if the dense jungle of plants were there for a reason other than their beauty. Maybe for protection, maybe as a weapon, or maybe it was both.

Soon after we reemerged into the sunlight, we arrived at the modest two-story bungalow that housed Solon's office. Klive parked behind the lawyer's modest Toyota and cut the engine of his truck, watching me with laughing cerulean eyes. "Scared, Oswin?"

"No," I answered truthfully. I wasn't scared, per se, just nervous. Was I really doing the right thing by coming here? It was vital that I make the right decision for the pack. There was no turning back once I went through with this.

"If you're not scared, then why are you still sitting here?" he asked.

"I guess I'm wondering if this is crazy, Klive."

He shook his head as if it would repel my words, his expression serious for once in his short life. "It's been three years, boss. What's crazy is that you've been able to stay away from her for this long without losing your marbles."

I sighed. "You're right. I know you're right."

Being away from Korrina was torture. So many of my nights were spent thinking of her, reminiscing about the feel of her beautiful dark hair in my hands, her perfect mouth on mine, the absolute amazement of seeing her in her natural form as she writhed in pleasure beneath me. And when I wasn't lying awake with the emptiness eating me alive, I was dreaming of her, reliving every second we'd been together in exaggerated color, sound, and acrobatics. At least, I think it was exaggerated. After three years, I could barely remember the real version of my mate.

Klive sized me up and raised a blond brow. "Am I going to have to drag you out of the truck?"

Our heads jerked to a flutter of movement in the front window, bringing our attention back to the house. "Don't bother. It looks like we've been discovered."

He rolled his eyes. "Of course, we have. You've been out here gathering wool for three minutes. Get out of the truck, Oswin, or you might get caught being a coward."

"I'm kicking your ass when we're done here."

He smiled sweetly. "I look forward to it."

Klive could be an ass, but damn if that ass wasn't right. Solon might be a very old nymph, but he was still as spritely as a young human. That meant I had no more than five seconds to decide. It was time to face my fears or turn tail and run.

Sighing again, I stole a quick glance in the sun visor's mirror. It showed the same anxiety-ridden, desperate wolf that I'd been staring at for the last three years or so, same blonde hair—same blue-green eyes, same dead expression in those eyes. Yeah, this couldn't wait any longer. I had to get the ball rolling on getting my mate back today.

Before I could finish my internal pep talk, Solon appeared on his doorstep. He smiled broadly as he waited for me to scramble out of the truck. "Mr. Morris!" he exclaimed, shaking my hand. "You took longer than I expected."

"How so?" I asked, confused by his clandestine smile and unusually eager body language.

Solon raised his black eyebrows in surprise. "You have come to get Korrina back, haven't you?"

Aha. He knew precisely why I'd come. "Yes, sir, I have. The pack needs their Alpha female. We're almost thirty strong now."

He nodded sagely. "I see. Come on in, and we'll get the paperwork started. You know, in case Korrina hasn't changed in the last three years."

I chuckled. "Somehow, I don't think that's likely to have happened."

"No doubt you're going to be right about that," he agreed, his green eyes twinkling as he led me to the door.

I waved to Klive before I went inside. He wasted no time in kicking his feet up on the dash and taking out a book. That was Klive, always on the lookout for trouble. As a second, Klive Williams was about as ferocious as pet lamb, but I couldn't ask for someone more loyal. He was all business when it came to protecting the pack. With eight sisters to think about, he had no choice.

Solon's office was as I expected, spotless and filled with books. The male was renown in the supernatural community as the most educated, well-liked of the group and was a shoo-in for the next Bureau head. He had experience as a lawyer and a judge, the knowledge to be precise in his decisions, and the reputation of being on the up and up, which, let's be honest, is hard to find among the preternatural set.

"Have a seat, Oswin. Whiskey?" he asked, offering me an amber liquid that was no doubt aged to perfection.

"No, thanks," I declined, taking a seat in the brown leather armchair in front of his desk. "I'm leaving Meadowbrook as soon as we're done here."

"Good answer, my friend, a very responsible choice." He brought the bottle with him, sat across from me, and toasted in my direction. "To the pack."

"Thanks." I inclined my head in appreciation. "About the pack, Solon, I want you to know that I'm not doing this lightly. I know what I did to Korrina was inexcusable, and I don't expect her to forgive me. I don't forgive me." I paused, searching for the right words. "It's just that the pack needs more direction—direction I can't provide. They need their Alpha female."

Solon smiled serenely and poured himself another drink. "Historically, the strongest packs have had a female to help share the task. Do not be ashamed that you want the best for your new pack."

"Then you'll represent me?" I asked, not willing to waste another second here if he was going to refuse to help.

"Of course, I will," Solon said, an encouraging smile lighting up his somber face. "Korrina may be my favorite niece, but she signed up for this duty. That means she's obligated to see it through." There was a pregnant pause before he continued. "Forgive me if I'm overstepping my boundaries, but is it safe to say that there's been a fair amount of emotional distress caused by the absence of your mate?"

"Every day without her is like living with half of myself," I admitted. "Ever since I left her in Obsidian's care, I've craved her like nothing else. And I know she wants me as much as I want her. The seductive allure of her call through our bond torments my wolf. It's a bone-deep yearning, Judge Manetas. The temptation of the invocation is rivaled only by the full moon."

In understanding, he nodded. "Oswin, you have a case here, and moreover, I think that you are right to force her into her shirked responsibility. Regardless of the ... less than ideal circumstances between you two, there is still a pack to consider. She knew when she mated you that the deal was ironclad, irreversible."

"Judge Manetas, I think I might kiss you."

Bemused, he said, "That's completely unnecessary, Mr. Morris," and reached into the file cabinet next to his desk. He selected a single sheet of paper from a file folder and handed it to me. "All I need you to do is fill out this form and wait for the wrath that should be coming your way in a couple days."

"I'm scared already," I said. It was sad, but that wasn't a lie. Korrina could be a force to be reckoned with.

Chuckling, Solon poured himself a third drink, this time a double. "You should be. We both should be. Korrina will not thank us for this, especially after her latest annulment request was denied by the Bureau so recently. You realize she's married Obsidian Raines in a human court to spite you, don't you?"

Sighing, I said, "I expected no less," and read over the paperwork. I filled out a couple of lines before the questions I'd wanted to ask since my arrival burst from my lips. "How is she, Solon? Is she happy? Is this going to ruin her life?"

Solon sat back in his chair and exhaled. "You have no idea how happy and successful she's been in the past couple of years. She and Obsidian started a truffle business shortly after her change, and only recently, they've bought a home in Everlast. They've done extremely well for themselves."

"Everlast?" I asked. "The vampire community in Virginia that was on the news a couple months ago?"

"The very one." He pursed his lips and took another sip of whiskey. "The victim of that awful crime is one of Korrina's closest friends. Your mate saved that young woman's life ... so to speak."

Now everything was starting to make sense. I had always pined for Korrina; that was an everyday thing. But this past winter, the longing had become so intense, I thought about driving to Goshen every day to be closer to her. My wolf had sensed the distance. Leave it to him to notice the things I never took the time to.

When I continued to keep quiet with my thoughts, Solon said, "Don't worry, pack-master. We'll get your female back where she belongs. I just hope you're ready for Obsidian to come with her. She won't leave him behind, and according to your laws, she doesn't have to."

My jaw clenched tight at the thought, but it wasn't as if I hadn't already considered the situation from every angle. "I know the risks. I have to get her back. At this point, I'll probably agree to anything she asks."

Solon stood. "Then get her back, we shall. She'll try to fight it, and she may even call you directly to try to sweet talk you into dropping your case. Don't. Threaten her with the Bureau if you must. Hopefully, she'll listen to me and not want to escalate this to a preceding. That's our best hope … for now.

"Do you think it's likely she'll listen?" I asked.

He rounded his desk and clapped me on the shoulder in commiseration. "After you've refused her requests for an annulment five times? Not a chance in hell, Oswin. Not a chance in hell."

# MY LIFE RUINED

## KORRINA

*Monday, March 13th*

*It feels like it's been ages since I last wrote, journal. I guess I haven't had anything to write about. The truffle business is booming, Obsidian and I bought a house in what I'm now referring to as Paranormal Park Place, and I'm finally getting used to having fangs. There's not much to complain about when you're deliriously happy.*

*K*

"*My life is perfect,*" I thought as I stared up at the stars.

Well, it would be perfect if Obsidian would get back with the wine. I could really use another drink … or four.

Relaxing back on the grass, I enjoyed a few blissful minutes of silence before Santiago's Waltz from the Interview with a Vampire soundtrack blared from my phone. I groaned. Alexis was relentless.

Alexis, albeit a very good friend and one of the most caring women I'd ever known, was driving everyone in her life to the brink of insanity with her insatiable 'new vampire' bloodlust. For two solid weeks, she'd begged for more blood than her new husband, Tobias, would allow, and when she wasn't begging him or our mutual bestie, Sapphire, she was driving me up a wall. Alexis had little self-control in life, so we understood that we'd be in for a ride after her change, but nobody expected that ride to be so long … with no rest stops.

"Sapphire?" I nudged my saintly brunette friend with a foot. She was laying in the grass with me, staring up at the moon. "Whose turn is it?"

"Mine," she said, exhaling a loud, world-weary sigh. As if on cue, The Vampire Diaries theme song erupted from her phone. She aimed a death glare at the screen and punched ignore. "Remind me why we're friends with Alexis, again?"

"Because she has all the charm and looks of a cherubic angel and is just absurd enough to be friend-worthy?" I asked.

Sapphire laughed. "That sounds about right."

"Oh, and let's not forget her husband's accent is smoking hot." I sighed. "So, so very hot."

Sapphire shook her head. "I'm going to text Obsidian and tell him his wife is a drunken slut."

"A drunken slut that's right!" I said, giggling at the two of her. "And you almost had sex with him! Lucky!"

She threw an arm over her eyes. "Don't remind me!"

"Are you kidding? If I saw Tobias Faust naked, I would think of it daily. Maybe, hourly."

"Married, mated, and thinking about other males? You are such a nymph!"

I snickered. "That may be the worst attempt at an insult ever."

"Forgive me, I'm drunk and not on my 'A' game."

"I know how you feel," I said, grinning at her. "And you know what? It feels nice." I rose my arms above my head and rolled in grass that plumped as I touched it. The plants loved it when I made contact with them. They were happy to play along with my silliness.

Sapphire relaxed next to me and powered down her phone. "You're right. It does feel nice. And you know what else? I think sexy-man Tobias is on his own tonight. He's her maker, after all. He can compel her to drink less blood. It's the only thing that makes sense. I don't care about his noble sensibilities. She's out of control."

"Second that," I said sourly.

She tipped her wine glass at me and grinned. "I knew you would."

"To doing questionable things to your spouse!" I slurred, lifting my glass for a toast. Over the rim, I saw the tall, dark, and handsome vampire I'd made my husband exit the back door. "Finally! You're home! I thought I was going to have to send out a search party!"

"What questionable things are you two talking about?" my husband asked, looking wary.

"Obsidian, you won't believe what your wife said!" Sapphire tattled. "The old slut!"

I glared at her. "Old slut? I stopped aging at twenty-eight!"

"I stopped at twenty-two, therefore…"

"You mean, vindictive old slut," I said, snatching the glass from her hand and rolling away when she tried to get it back.

"My love, we have a guest," Obsidian said, stepping aside to reveal an amused Uncle Solon.

"Solon!" I exclaimed, drunkenly scrambling up to greet him.

With his usual loving smile, he accepted the tight hug I gave him and leaned down to give me a smacking kiss on the top of my head. "How's my favorite niece tonight?"

"Great! Sapphire, this is my Uncle Solon. Solon, this is Sapphire. She's married to Kieran Kinane."

"Congratulations on a fine conquest," he told my wobbly friend.

Sapphire made a valiant attempt to stand but was ultimately unsuccessful. "Thanks. Sorry, I'd shake your hand, but I seem to be having technical difficulties at the moment."

Solon smiled at us, the few strands of silver in his black hair shimmering merrily in the moonlight. "Perhaps, we should join you in the grass. You two seem to be a few drinks ahead of us."

"You're sleeping over?" I asked, excited at the prospect. I knew Solon wouldn't drink and drive, and we'd never had any family stay at our beautiful new house. He was the perfect first guest.

"If that's okay. I don't want to impose, but it is a long drive back to Meadowbrook."

I poured him a glass of Pinot Grigio, delighted to hand my uncle a decent glass of wine in the expensive stemware Kieran gave us for a housewarming present. "Of course, it's all right! We'd love to have you."

"You'd better ask Obsidian about that," Sapphire said. "Unless you guys started a game of facial charades I was too drunk to notice, I think he has something on his mind."

I looked to my husband, who was indeed trying to convey something in his expression. "Spit it out, Obsidian."

He sighed. "Forgive me for my rudeness, old friend, but what are you doing here?"

Solon laughed at his unabashed way of getting to the point. "You're right to be suspicious. I'm not here on a social call. Obsidian, Korrina, we have a major issue."

"Oswin?" we asked in unison.

"The very werewolf," he answered, gauging our reactions with interest. "He is insisting on your return to the pack."

Shaken, I sat down in the patio chair across from him. "What does this mean, Solon?"

"Guys," Sapphire interjected, sounding far soberer than she'd been minutes before. "This feels like my cue to leave. I'll see you tomorrow night, Korrina?"

"Okay," I answered, too distracted by the current crisis to see her out. What was Oswin trying to do? He left me, not the other way around.

12

Solon sighed and took my hand. "You should call your Realtor."

"What?" I watched as the hibiscus climbing up the stuccoed back wall of my townhouse wilted upon hearing the news. "I can't leave Everlast. I won't leave."

"Then you may want to obtain an attorney licensed in the state of Alabama. You'll be needing one."

Eyes wide, I realized what he was saying. "You won't be representing us?"

"I'm sorry, no. I'm the opposing counsel."

Obsidian wrapped his arms around me from behind as bloody tears pricked at my eyes. "How could you, Solon?"

"Very easily. Oswin asked, and I accepted."

"But ... why?"

"Because we are on a losing side," Obsidian answered for him.

"Exactly," Solon said. "Korrina, in all the years you've known me, have I ever taken a case I knew I couldn't win?" He placed his big hand over my small one. "Honey, I would have taken yours, if you had a leg to stand on. You mated Oswin with full knowledge of what that meant. As long as he is Alpha of a wolf pack, you are his Alpha female."

"Wait a sec." I broke out of Obsidian's hold to fill my glass with the remnants of the opened bottle of wine and downed it. "Let me get this straight. You want me to sell the house that we just bought, with a loan that took us two long years to acquire, so we can move back to Alabama to live with a pack that doesn't have a permanent home and a male that left me on my deathbed, all because I had the audacity to get stabbed to death by one of his psychotic wolves?"

Solon squeezed my hand and pursed his lips, before saying, "I'm sorry, Korrina. That is the sum of it, yes."

"Well, fuck." What else was there to say? My temporary happiness was officially over.

*** 

As soon as Solon was tucked in and snoring away in the guest room for the night, I fled to my favorite spot in the house. The sunroom, or solarium as Obsidian called it, was the one place we couldn't be overheard by others in the house or by our neighbors. It was our sanctum, our place for peace and solitude, even in the day, thanks to modern technology.

Obsidian was already waiting for me when I walked in. He kept his expression neutral, a blatant attempt to keep me calm, but he held out his arms, knowing I'd need solace. "Come here, my love."

I climbed into his lap and tucked my head beneath his chin, a motion I'd made so many times it was familiar, soothing to me. "Obsidian, what are we going to do?"

"We will sell the house and move to Oswin's new pack-lands," he said matter-of-factly. "I know you don't want to hear this, but if Solon has no hope for us to win, then neither do I. We should accept the inevitable and move on to planning our future wherever we end up. We have business concerns to take care of— new licenses, new business cards, advertising in a new market— there are a million little things to do on top of selling this house."

I glared up at him. "You are such a fucking quitter."

He cupped my jaw and kissed me with a glimmer of humor in his amber eyes. "Korrina, I might remind you that we knew this day could come. We made the decision for you to mate Oswin together, fully aware of the consequences, and we must stand by it. It's the right thing to do."

Distraught, I stared at him for a few moments. I'd expected him to feel like me—completely and totally lost. "How can you be so damn calm and reasonable about all of this?" I asked, perplexed by his emotionless response to losing our home.

"You mean, besides the fact that I am calm and reasonable? Well, for one, we've had three years to make peace with the fact that we could, and most likely would, be forced to go back to the pack-lands. Two, unlike you, I'm not hammered."

"Don't try to make me laugh!" I scolded, moving out of his lap before hysterical, bloody tears made an appearance. "I haven't made my peace with this. I like my life here. Everyone I love is here."

He raised a brow. "Everyone?"

"You know what I mean, Obsidian. You can be a well-adjusted adult if you want to, but me? Hell no. This is like some horrible dream I can't wake up from." I sighed. "One big-ass, never-ending, wolf-shaped nightmare."

Bemused, Obsidian shook his dark head and pressed his soft lips to my cheek. "Aren't you done wallowing in your woes yet? I thought you'd be on to anger by now. Seething with rage is a look that better suits you."

"Again, with the jokes?" I griped. "Can't you go back to the dry, humorless bastard I met almost four years ago, just for tonight? Please?"

Obsidian settled back into the cushions. "We'll be happy again, my love. It doesn't matter where we are, as long as we're together."

"I don't believe you," I said, staring up at the stars through the glass. "I feel like I'll never be happy again."

I felt him laugh into my hair, before saying, "I haven't had any trouble making you happy over the past three or so years."

Pushing his wandering hands from my breasts, I hissed, "We can't. Solon is here."

"He can't hear us," he argued, sliding his hands up until he cupped my breasts again. "He's asleep."

Sighing, I pressed myself into his palms. I couldn't deny him. "This isn't going to fix anything, you know."

"You're right," he agreed, pulling my sweater over my head. "But it will take your mind off the problem at hand for a few minutes."

He had a point there. When he touched me, there was nothing else but him. Nothing but his skin against mine, his fingers caressing my— "Okay, let's do this," I told him, yanking the straps of my dress down to expose my breasts. "But we'll continue this conversation later."

"Not if I fuck you into incoherency."

Slipping off my panties, I moved to the end of the couch and spread my legs. "Do your damnedest, Obsidian."

# IT'S REALLY HAPPENING
## OSWIN

I couldn't remember a single time in recent memory that I was more nervous than I was right now. How could a female make me feel like a pup on his first run? Me, Oswin Morris, an Alpha wolf running scared from his own mate? What was my world coming to?

"Are you okay over there?" Solon asked me again. I think my twitchiness was making him jumpy.

"I'm good," I assured him. "Just anxious to see her."

He didn't look convinced. I wouldn't be either, not with the way I was staring a hole in the small table in front of me. But how could I not be on edge right now? In a few seconds, Korrina would be sitting across from me. My mate, my everything, would be within arm's reach, and I couldn't touch her. I didn't know if my wolf could handle it. The sound of their car turning off the main road had him clawing at my skin to get out.

Solon rushed to his feet with an encouraging smile plastered to his face when he heard the crunch of gravel in front of the house. I, on the other hand, frantically straightened my tie, ran a hand through my hair, and tried to appear calm. It wasn't easy. I could already smell her familiar earthy scent from where I sat.

A few moments and murmured hellos later, my mate entered the room. I shot to my feet as she and Obsidian followed Solon into the room. "Korrina," I breathed out, unable to stop myself. She was so much more beautiful than I remembered. Had her dark hair always shone in the light like that? Had her eyes always been that green?

"Oswin," she replied coolly, taking the seat furthest away from where I sat.

Brushing off her cold response, I asked Obsidian, "How are you, brother?" and stuck out my hand, praying he would make this easy on me and take it.

"I'm well, Oswin," he answered, taking my hand and trying to warn me of something with his eyes. "How's the new pack treating you?"

"Very well," I told the handsome vampire, relieved that he was being friendly and covertly helpful, but then again, I hadn't expected any other reaction from Obsidian. He'd always been semi-level-headed, even when he was unhappily married to my sister.

"No major problems?"

"Not a one," I said proudly. "Fresh blood seems to have calmed the problems that plagued the Thomasville pack."

"Well, you are wolves," Korrina muttered under her breath. Obviously, she wouldn't be employing her husband's friendly tactic.

"Be a lady!" Solon scolded, tutting her bad behavior as he motioned for the rest of us to sit. "And where is your council?"

"I don't need a lawyer, Uncle Solon. What's the point? Someone hasn't given me a choice in the matter."

My mate aimed her angry gaze at me, and my erection sprang to attention of its own volition. Wincing, I ignored the incredibly uncomfortable pinch of my jeans and told Solon, "As long as she intends on coming back to the pack-lands, I don't think we'll need to get the courts involved."

"Don't you mean the Thomasville Comfort Inn?" she asked, her voice dripping with sarcasm. "I hear that's where you're keeping your new pack."

"Only for the interim, darlin'," I said, disregarding Obsidian's slight shake of his head.

I probably should have heeded his caution; her hatred for me was an ugly, tangible thing between us now, and Obsidian had been front and center to bear witness to every moment she'd had to sharpen her anger into weapons capable of causing me pain, but I couldn't. Apparently, I was a glutton for punishment.

"You know," I said, meeting her gaze. "I think that even a nymph would agree that the Comfort Inn is better than a sleeping bag and a tent in the woods."

She rolled her grass green eyes. "Yeah, but what's beyond that, Oswin? Where will we live permanently?"

"Allow me to make a suggestion," Obsidian said, interrupting the terse volley of our conversation. "To me, the obvious choice is Goshen. You own a huge amount of land right next to mine. There's plenty of room for a growing pack."

"That idea has merit," Solon said, joining Obsidian in his quest to keep the situation civil. "It will certainly solve your space problem."

I'd thought of the Goshen property before. It certainly made the most sense. However, the cost could run up into the millions. I couldn't sink my life savings into something that could go the same way my first pack went. I took great strides to keep my financial future secure. When you're practically immortal, you must.

"I'm not so sure I can afford it," I told them. "The cost of clearing and building would be astronomical."

"You could, if the nymphs help you," Solon countered. "Don't forget that your mate has a huge family, some with very powerful connections. If now isn't the time to exploit those connections, I don't know when is. And it would be nothing for us to ask the trees to move aside. Some trees might even volunteer for lumber. With that and the pack's help, I reckon you could be up and running in six months' time."

I nodded in full agreement. "I'm all for it if that's what my mate wants."

"Your mate wants to go home to Virginia and forget this week ever happened," Korrina snapped. "How fucking dare you do this to me? You abandoned me. You didn't want me. Why are you doing this now?"

As I watched my mate dissolve into tears, I knew, without a doubt, that I was the worst creature on the planet. What kind of asshole does this after three full years of no contact? It was as if I gave her just enough time to get used to life without me then ambushed her.

"Well?" she prompted.

"You're my mate," I answered simply. "To live without you is impossible, and … I love you. I never stopped loving you."

I had to hand it to Obsidian. He took the news in his usual calm stride, whereas Korrina looked like she was about to lose her shit. I could practically roast a marshmallow over the hot, molten heat of the fury roiling off her.

She stood up from the table, and everyone followed suit. No one dared do anything different. "I have demands," she said. "If they aren't met, I won't do this." She looked me in the eye, daring me to say no.

"Let's have them," I said, then nodded at Solon to make amendments to the paperwork if need be.

Korrina counted her conditions off on her fingers. "First, Obsidian is my husband. I will spend every night with him at his house until I deem you worthy of my private company, assuming that ever happens. I make zero guarantees on that."

"I understand," I told her. "I expected no less."

"Second," she continued, ignoring my statement altogether. "Don't think I'll be friendly, or complacent, or nice, or that I will ever love you again. I don't trust you and probably never will."

I nodded. What else could I do? Lord knows I would agree to anything to get her back in my life.

"And third, I want a year to move back to Goshen."

"Six months," I bargained. I couldn't bear the thought of waiting another year.

"Seven months," Korrina countered.

Her tenacity made me grin. "Done."

She smiled back before she caught herself, then she glared at me for causing it. "See you in seven months, Mr. Morris."

I watched her take an apologetic Obsidian's arm, and they walked out the door together without looking back.

"Seven months," I said to myself.

Once they were in the car, Solon clapped me on the back. "I'd like to tell you that the hard part is over, but I don't like to lie."

"That may be true, Solon," I said. "But at least, it's something, and something is more than I had ten minutes ago."

***

When I pulled into the driveway of the Comfort Inn after the meeting, I guided my truck into the closest parking space and sat there in pure disbelief. Korrina was coming home. I would have my mate back. Seven months didn't leave me a lot of time to build the new pack-lands, but I didn't care. I would make it work. I would do anything for her.

A tap on the window broke the focus I had on my bleak future. I pried my stiff hands off the steering wheel and glanced over, finding Klive smiling questioningly at me, his head tilted at a 'what the fuck are you doing?' angle.

"Hey, boss," he said through the glass. "Are you going to be in there all day, or are you going to get your ass out here and tell me what happened?"

I opened the door and stepped out into the chilly night air, closing the door behind me. "We're moving," I told him gruffly. "That's what happened."

His eyebrows shot up. "Oh, yeah? Where?"

"Goshen."

"Where's that?"

"About an hour south of Montgomery. It won't be hard to find work there or around Enterprise. Hell, even Mobile isn't that far of a haul."

"Okay, so why Goshen?"

"I own a few thousand acres next door to the familial estates that belong to Korrina's husband. He actually suggested we build there."

Klive nodded. "Well, at least, he's on board with her coming back to the pack. But, uh, where are we going to live while we're there?"

"We'll stay at a local hotel while we build. I want every couple and single person to be in their own homes in seven months' time."

He whistled low. "Ain't it going to be a little pricey for that many houses? What is that? Twenty-five or thirty? Are you sure you can swing that amount?"

I shrugged. "It's time to do something permanent. Your sisters won't stay single forever, you know. They'll need a house for their pups soon enough."

"Thanks for that," Klive said. He grimaced. "I totally needed to have nightmares about pale pink bunting and dirty diapers for the next week."

I clapped him on the back as we started for the entrance. "I'm going to have the plans done by the end of the week. This is on a real fast track."

"Got it. Just let me know what we'll need. I'll get the cement and lumber squared away with our suppliers. Oh, and we'll have to hire someone to clear the land."

"We're going to have to do a field survey first. Manetas is a nymph. He said he could get most of the trees to relocate for us upon request. He also said that some might sacrifice themselves for the lumber if they're ready to go."

My second stared at me. "That's fucking hardcore."

"Yeah, and so was Korrina. She was sitting at that table like a caged viper, a very pissed off viper. I was expecting anger; that was a given, but what I just experienced from her was way, way past anger. She took every opportunity to strike at me."

Klive shrugged. "What did you expect her to be like?"

"To be honest, with Korrina, I try not to have too many expectations. She always exceeds them. Sometimes, in the positive. Sometimes, in the negative."

"Sounds like you have a pretty interesting mate to contend with."

I shook my head and laughed. "Klive, you have no idea."

***

It was only after two days of honest to God freaking out did I put on my big boy pants and broach the subject with the pack. In that short space of time, I learned two things for sure. One, Klive could keep a secret like nobody's business. And two, I was a fucking coward. I was terrified to upset the delicate balance of the pack. They were happy in Thomasville, content. I didn't want to change that.

In the end, all my worrying was for not. Most of the pack were delighted with the news. They were excited to finally have a real home, even if it didn't have daily maid service. It was the kids that took the news the hardest, and they certainly weren't shy about making their displeasure known. It took quite a bit of persuading and a not so subtle reminder that their parents were tired of using quarters to do their laundry before they were truly reconciled with the idea.

A few days after the announcement, the move seemed to be becoming a reality. I had the plans, permits, and supplies for the build. What I didn't have was a crew. All my guys were on other long-term jobs and wouldn't be done for at least two months or more. I considered asking another builder to bid on the job, but I had serious doubts I'd get a reasonable price from my competitors. I'd underbid them enough that they would probably jump at the chance to screw me over, especially with a deadline like this. Never mind that it was their own fault for being greedy and bilking their 'deer in the headlights' clients out of more of their hard-earned money than the work was worth.

At my wit's end, I picked up my phone. "Call Klive," I said with a sigh.

There wasn't even a ring before Klive asked, "What's up?" in lieu of a greeting.

"How are your sisters at swinging a hammer?"

He laughed. "They taught me everything I know. Why?"

"Because we need a crew for a couple of months. Do you think they could handle it with the rest of the adults?"

"I think they'll need someone to corral them, but yeah, they can do it."

I sighed in relief. "Good. Let them know. We'll check in at the Holiday Inn tomorrow and break ground the next day."

"I'll do that," he said with humor in his voice. Seeing me try and fail to keep his impertinent sisters in line would be the highlight of his year.

"Thanks. See you later."

"Later."

I hung up the phone and stared at the grove of pines outside my office window. It would be the last time I did. Tomorrow, all of this would be in Goshen, and I'd begin the next phase of my life. I prayed it would go smoothly. So much depended on this move being a success.

# I MUST PROTECT HER

## OBSIDIAN

## *SIX AND A HALF MONTHS LATER*

"Obsidian, do you have to go to Italy tonight?" Korrina asked. She was sitting in the middle of the bed, clutching two cushy Hampton Inn pillows to her chest as if they'd console her. It was adorable, really.

I bent to give her a peck on the cheek. "My love, you know I have to. This trip has been planned for two years. And you made a promise to Solon," I reminded her. "You have to see this through. It's time."

"Can't we stay here another night? Just one more?"

Her semi-hopeful pout became a genuinely unhappy one when she noticed I was wearing my 'this is going to happen whether you like it or not' face. She hated that face. "I'm starting to think you're trying to get rid of me," she said petulantly.

"No chance, sweetheart." I sat next to her, plucked the pillows from her lap, and pulled her into my arms. "I will never leave you, Korrina ... because you can't buy back your soul from the devil." She protested by giving me a playful smack. "Really! Do try to control yourself!" I teased. That, of course, prompted another swat. "Okay," I said, lifting her up to straddle my lap. "I think someone is afraid of the big bad wolf."

"Don't even," she started before I put my finger over her lips.

"Everything is going to be fine. We've talked this out dozens of times. After the trip to Italy, I can be around anytime or anywhere you have need of me."

Suspicious, she raised her brows. "Why do you sound so sure about that?"

A mischievous smile spread across my face. "Solon told me Oswin doesn't have a choice. Consorts, of any species, are allowed on the pack-lands."

"When did you talk to him about this?"

"Last week … and in August … and in April. To tell you the truth, we haven't stopped talking about it since the meeting."

"Thanks for telling me," she grumbled. I knew she was resisting the urge to smack me again.

"Korrina, I assumed you knew I would. You've been studying up on this. I want to be prepared, too."

"Yeah, but do you and my uncle have to have super-secret meetings about it behind my back? I'm not hiding my studying from you."

"One, it wasn't super-secret. It was a meeting between two old friends. And two, Solon knows more about pack laws and werewolf lore than anyone on the planet. No one has insight into this kind of dilemma like he does."

"Still," she said, more than a little miffed about the secrecy.

I sighed. "I only did it as a precaution. Having vampires in a werewolf pack is sure to be a little precarious—for Oswin and for us. I need to know how to protect you from them if the need arises."

"Oh. I hadn't thought of myself as a vampire in this situation, or really, any situation. That's not what I am. Yes, I have to drink a little blood occasionally, but I can walk in the sun and eat just like anyone else. The term 'vampire' doesn't define me, not even close." She paused, looking like a scared little mouse. "We should have talked about this more," she said, not able to keep the whine out of her voice. "I'm worried about the 'what ifs'."

"When have you ever cared about the rules or being prepared?"

She feigned thought. "Never?"

I grinned. "Exactly. So, are you ready to check out?"

She blanched as a moment of sheer panic followed my question. "Can I do this, Obsidian? Am I ready to do this?"

"You're overthinking this," I told her, cupping her beautiful heart-shaped face. "We don't know what it will be like until we get there. Let's not start worrying until there's something to worry about, okay?"

"Why are you so rational about this? Don't you feel overwhelmed, like everything is out of your control?"

I pressed my lips against hers for a long moment, then said, "You have been in control of my heart for almost four years. Every day I feel overwhelmed that you chose to be my bride. And even if our relationship is never without obstacles, it will always be worth it. Korrina, to me, you are worth any amount of struggle."

"Well, of course, I'm worth it," she sassed. "You, on the other hand, I'm still not sure why I keep you around."

I dumped her off my lap and quickly covered her body with mine. "Do I need to remind you why you keep me around, again?"

"It couldn't hurt," she told me, keeping her voice bored and disaffected. "I barely remember what sex is like, it's been so long."

"It was three hours ago, you insatiable nymph."

Affronted, she started to unleash what I was sure would be a worthy tirade, but I stole the retort from her lips with a deep, searching kiss that made her whole body come alive with desire. Breaking the kiss, I rose to my knees and slowly loosened my tie as I looked over her body with focused, hungry eyes. "I'll postpone my flight until tomorrow, no longer," I told her.

"Good," she said, reaching to unbuckle my belt. "I want you inside of me."

"What a coincidence," I said, my fangs peeking out of my mouth as I smiled down at her. "That is exactly where I want to be."

She palmed my erection and gave it a light squeeze. "That is a coincidence."

I shuddered and pulled my shirt over my head. "Careful, Korrina."

"Why? Is some vampire going to come after me for doing this?"

"No," I corrected, speaking through clenched teeth. "Some vampire is going to come before you if you keep doing that."

She laughed and released her grip. "I'd prefer you do that after my panties are off."

My cock jumped in anticipation as my gaze roamed from the red silk shelf bra down to the matching panties she wore. "Allow me to take care of that."

"Be my guest," she said, her voice husky with want.

I sat back on my heels and leisurely trailed the tips of my fingers down her body, starting at her shoulders, working my way down over her taut nipples to curl my fingers in the tiny scrap of damp fabric that covered her. With a firm tug, I ripped the material apart and grinned winsomely when she let out a surprised gasp. "I like that sound," I growled.

"I like it when you make me make that sound," she purred, arching against my rock-hard cock. "Make me do it again."

She didn't have to ask twice. I moved into her slick entrance with uncustomary efficiency, my teeth clenched tight in restraint. Moaning, she dug her fingernails into my back as her body stretched to accommodate my size, making me hiss at the sharp pain and strike back, my control lost as I buried my fangs in her throat. She screamed and rocked against me as she came apart, expertly milking my cock to bring me to the edge with her. My mind went blank as orgasm roiled through me. My whole universe consisted of nothing but the wound I pulled blood from and the hard and fast rhythm of my dick inside her. For that one split second, my world consisted of nothing but my wife, nothing but my Korrina.

*\*\**

Korrina and I took an Uber to the airport, and after a somewhat hysterical, tearful goodbye, went our separate ways. Well, that was what Korrina thought we were doing. I didn't dare tell her what I really intended to do.

After I saw her off to her flight, I stepped around the corner of the terminal and turned to mist to speed toward the back-roads route I'd planned months ago. From there, I materialized to a semi-solid state and ran full out. The pack-lands were much farther than I'd ever ran before, and I knew I'd have to stop to feed on something that didn't come in a fancy prepackaged container, but it was a necessary trip. I wouldn't leave my wife in the hands of someone I couldn't trust.

For the first two hundred miles or so, I let my instincts guide me. I needed time to analyze the huge change of life I was about to embark on. I'd been taking so many precautions, doing what I could to make sure Korrina was protected, I hadn't taken much time to think about what my night to nightlife would be like. Would I be able to share my wife with Oswin now that I knew the amount of selfishness and vengeance he was capable of? Would I be able to handle seeing them together without trying to rip his head off? I suspected the answer depended on what he had to say to me when I got to Goshen tonight.

The hunger I'd dreaded started slowly, just an empty pang reminding me I'd have to feed soon. As always, I tried to ignore it. The thought of forcing a human to give me their blood was repellent. Not because of the crime or the theft but the way it made me feel. The feeling was a fallacy of power, one that made me imagine I was somehow more than the pitiful humans I stole my supper from like I was a god among them. I despised that feeling.

And so, I continued, running through town after town, until I could go no farther. Resigning myself to the fact that I desperately needed nourishment, I followed a beacon of glowing streetlights until I spied a stumbling, dark-haired drunk man coming out of a Waffle House restaurant on the outskirts of a small town. Perfect. He'd never know what hit him.

Running toward him at full speed, I knelt down between his car and the next one long before he staggered across the parking lot. When he rounded the bumper, I looked him in his surprised blue eyes and demanded, "Get in the car, unlock the passenger door, and uncover your neck. I'm going to feed from you."

Without any hesitation, he did as I asked. I slid into the seat next to him and wasted no time. His blood was rich and vibrant, unlike the diluted swill they mass produced by the six-pack. It was just what I needed to push through the last couple hundred miles to the pack-lands.

With my thirst slaked, I closed the wounds and told the man, "When I'm out of sight, lay down in the back seat and sleep it off. Don't remember anything about what I did and never get this drunk again."

"Okay," he said, looking dazed as he held his sleeve to his neck.

A second later, it was as if I never existed and I was back on my way.

*\*\**

It was an eerie feeling, walking into the heart of wolf territory. I knew without seeing them that every wolf was keenly aware of a vampire in their midst. Every single one of them. Nothing else could explain why my skin was crawling with the need to mist myself to safety. A vampire traipsing into a pack of wolves wasn't just stupid, it was fatal.

I found Oswin waiting on the front porch of the address he'd had given me months before. Obviously, he'd sensed my arrival like everyone else had. I hesitated in the shadows, trying to convince myself that I could handle the situation, should they attack. I was woefully outnumbered.

With a muttered, "Fuck it," I locked my eyes on the pack-master and brazenly stepped out into the street, only to be greeted by the growls and glowing eyes of a dozen angry wolves.

"Cut the shit!" Oswin barked, looking harassed. "He's a guest."

Oswin's reproach did the trick. I didn't hear so much as a yip as he met me halfway across the street and shook my hand before leading me into the house. It appeared that he reigned supreme once more. That was a giant-sized relief.

The look of question in his expression said everything Oswin didn't when he closed the door behind us and faced me. I smiled at the wolf that was once my brother-in-law. "I thought I'd pay you a visit before Korrina arrives in a couple hours."

He stiffened, his yellow wolf eyes gleaming. "Something you'd like to say, brother?"

"Relax," I told him. "I'm not going to cause trouble. I only thought you might want to know what to expect before she gets here."

"Oh," he said, ratcheting down his animosity a few thousand notches. "Want a drink? I've got blood."

Taken aback, I asked, "You went to the supermarket?"

"Well, yeah. I wanted to be prepared for Korrina's needs." He shook his head in disbelief. "I still can't believe they sell blood in the refrigerated aisle. It was right next to the organic milk. I never thought I'd see the day."

Oh, man. Korrina was going to eat this contrite, desperate version of Oswin alive. "Oswin, I hate to tell you this, but Korrina won't drink the bottled stuff."

His eyes widened at the implication. "You mean she drinks from humans?"

"She drinks from me."

He nodded and handed me a bottle of high dollar blood. "I'm not surprised. She's never been the kind of female that would hurt someone on purpose." Touching the small scar on his neck, he added, "Unless, it's deserved."

"This is a nice house," I said, changing the subject. I didn't want to reminisce about the night Korrina lost her life right now—or ever.

"Think she'll like it?" he asked hopefully.

I smiled at my old friend/enemy. "To put it bluntly, hell no. She'll hate everything about this place, anything you touch." In a serious tone, I added, "Oswin, you've no idea the depth of her hatred for you."

"Tell me," Oswin demanded, desperation tingeing his voice.

"I'm not sure she'll ever forgive you. Korrina isn't just angry; she's retaliatory."

A deep furrow marred his deceptively youthful-looking forehead. "How can I sway her?"

"I've been thinking a lot about that," I said, swallowing the last remnants of blood. "I think there might be a way."

He latched onto that tiniest bit of hope like he was a drowning man and I had the only life preserver in town. "How?"

I sat and sighed, hating what I was about to say. "Oswin, I may be Korrina's husband, but you are her mate. She'll never admit this to us, but she needs you. The distance from you torments her. It's painfully obvious, though she tries damn hard to hide it from me."

"So, what you're saying is…"

"She wants you. Play nice, and she'll come around. If not because of the mating, because of the sex. I'm going to be gone for days. She'll get the urge to fuck soon enough."

He raised his brows. "Are you telling me to try to seduce your wife?"

"No, I'm telling you to try to seduce your mate."

Bewildered, he asked, "And that's it? That's your advice?"

"Korrina is a social, curious creature. She will crave simulation of some sort within the first day. Put on that charm that got half of Edith's bridesmaids to sleep with you, and you'll be fine."

"Yeah, well, that was a long time ago. I'm old and mated now."

"One, you're not old. Don't give me that bullshit. And two, why should that matter? Have you seen your mate?"

A slow smile that made me want to kill him spread across his lips. "She does make those bridesmaids look like a pack of hyenas, doesn't she?"

"Fuck yeah, she does," I agreed. "But you don't have to sell me on her, Oswin, she has my heart."

He nodded in understanding but didn't comment.

"Look," I said, breaking a strenuous moment of silence. "If you think it will help, I won't call her for a few days when I get to Italy. I'll tell her I forgot my charger adapter or something. Use that time to your advantage."

Nervous now, Oswin's eyes shifted toward me then skittered away.

"Say what's on your mind, brother." God knows, he wasn't going to ask anything I hadn't prepared myself for in almost four years.

Oswin grinned. "Should've known you'd come right out with it. You've never been one to mince words."

"Indeed, I have not."

Oswin huffed through his nose—a very 'wolf' thing to do—before asking, "How can you do this, Obsidian?"

I sighed. "You're wondering how can I give up the one thing that means the most to me?"

"Yeah," he answered quietly.

Meeting him straight in the eye, I said, "I don't intend to. Korrina means more to me than sex and a pretty face. She loves me. That's a gift I've never been given before, even from your sister ... at least, not in the end, anyway. I don't intend on losing that. I know she can love us both."

Oswin was quiet for a full minute as he struggled his wolf for dominance. I knew hearing everything said in plain English would upset him. He would have to share, and aside from the occasional dalliance, that simply wasn't done in the pack. Mates were for life.

Finally regaining control, Oswin said, "My wolf hates you. He wants her to be his alone. But the man in me, he envies the love you have for each other. I want what you have."

I stood, confident that he was sincere. "Luckily for you, Oswin, you can have that. It can't be impossible. She forgave me when I was an asshole."

He shook his head and chuckled to himself. "That's true."

Smiling, I laid a hand on his shoulder. "Hang in there. It's going to be hell, but your bond will get you through."

"You think so?" he asked, hopeful again.

I gave him a commiserating pat on the back as I made my way to the door. "Call me if she does anything you think you can't handle, and ... uh, say a prayer or two. It can't hurt."

# A NEW HOME
## KORRINA

*Wednesday, September 26th*

*I have a secret, journal, a secret I'm ashamed of. Okay, here goes ...*

*I want Oswin Morris.*

*And what's worse? I think my husband knows about it. No, I know he does, and it's all my fault.*

*I find I can't stop mentioning Oswin in our conversations. In secret, I can't stop thinking about him, longing for him. It's insane. He hurt me in the worst way possible, and I seriously doubt that I could ever love him again, but I need him, crave him. What's wrong with me? I promised myself I'd forget him, just like I thought he'd forgotten me.*

*K*

The flight to Atlanta and the following taxi ride to Goshen took a little under six hours, getting me to my in-laws' house well before sunrise. I grabbed my overnight bag from the trunk, waved goodbye to Tim, the extremely chatty driver, and watched him speed away before stopping for a second to examine the house I'd lived in so long ago. It was every bit as formidable as it had been, despite the pleasant memory of a frantic Obsidian leaping up to the balcony to propose to me. That seemed like a lifetime ago now.

Once inside, I opened all the windows to air the place out and took my time unpacking the meager belongings I'd brought on the flight with me. The moving van wasn't scheduled to be here for another two days, so I wouldn't have much to do until then. Boredom was inevitable.

Restless, I wandered the house for a while, showered, and tried to get into the mood to reread Anne of Green Gables, but nothing could hold my attention—nothing but the pack-lands, that is. The need to see the finished product was overwhelming. My mind kept drifting back to the building plans I'd seen. I wanted to see how it compared in person, without an escort. There was no doubt in my mind that I would view the pack-lands differently if I saw Oswin beforehand. The second I saw his face; all my rational thinking abilities would disappear. Basically, I would want to Hulk out and use him as a giant hammer until I felt better. Honestly, it really was too bad that kind of thing was frowned upon.

I sighed and stood up from the chaise I'd been lounging on with new purpose. My mind was made up. I was going to go to the pack-lands before daybreak.

Pulling on a short satin robe, I slipped my feet into my favorite kitty slippers and set out from the house. At the edge of the yard, I gave a crepe myrtle a friendly pat and let my body turn to vapor, anxious to finally see what Oswin had done before any of the wolves woke.

With my misty vampire speed, it didn't take long to spy a huge stone-surrounded sign that boasted, *GOSHEN PACK-LANDS*, to anyone traveling down the isolated stretch of highway. The sign a definite surprise to see and a completely ballsy move. Though werewolves were out of the closet, so to speak, they weren't exactly welcomed graciously into human society. I was mystified as to why Oswin thought it was a good idea to advertise themselves so openly to the people of Goshen. Especially when some of the population still cleaned their shotguns on their front porches.

Shaking my head, I continued on my way until another emotion hit me. This one, I was more familiar with. The tiresome trip, the curiosity to see where I'd be serving as Alpha, and the surprise of the "deal with it, rednecks" sign made me forget how angry I was. But now that I was here, the emotion was as strong as it had ever been. And there could only be one reason for that; Oswin was close by. I could feel his presence like he was standing next to me. Try as I might to deny it, the bond was leading me right to his doorstep, the absolute last place I wanted to be.

To add serious insult to injury, my hope of hating the pack-lands was not turning out the way I'd wanted it to, at all. The community Oswin had created for his new pack was beyond anything I'd ever expected from him. For all intents and purposes, the new pack-lands was merely an upscale suburb, very much like Everlast, only with a vast tree-covered park in the center.

Slowly, I circled the park. It was dark and silent now, but I could imagine the pups pushing each other on the swings and playing hide and seek behind the many trees. Damn it. He'd outdone himself. Not that that, or anything Oswin had done since he decided to put on his Prince Charming costume made me feel any warmer towards him. Though it showed thoughtfulness, landscaping wasn't going to be the thing that would make me fall in love with him again. If that was even possible.

I moved on from the park, taking in the general splendor of the two-story houses, perfectly manicured lawns, and the gorgeous gas lamps lighting the way. Seeing the wolves putting their personal touches here and there, making it a home, was a stark difference from the way the vampires decorated in Everlast, but it felt good, right. It was just so quaint, so cozy, I could almost forgive Oswin for his terrible misconduct. Somehow, he'd managed to surprise us all and deliver everything he promised, though Obsidian and I didn't think he could … or would. But the proof really was in the pudding. He'd made good on his end of the bargain. Now I had to make good on mine.

Untroubled and actually kind of excited, I floated along until I found Oswin's pickup truck parked at the end of the street. I stopped short, almost afraid to move closer. Seeing his truck in front of what I was sure was "our" house seemed so final, like the end of something, and it made me nervous.

"Welcome, Korrina."

I had a moment of perfect panic as Oswin's voice raised goosebumps on my insubstantial skin. I spun to face him. While I was invisible, there was no doubt he knew exactly where I was. His gaze was so focused, it was as if he was looking into my soul, instead of the place my eyes would have been.

"Will you come inside the house?" he asked quietly, offering me an arm to usher me toward the two-story craftsman style house.

Ignoring the offer, I materialized and brushed past him to stomp up the front steps by myself. "You don't get to touch me, asshole."

He didn't deny being one. He only nodded to the yawning blond male that came out of the house next door and followed me in. "It doesn't have to be this way," he said softly. "I know we didn't leave on good terms, but we were happy once, weren't we, darlin'?"

"Happy?" I roared, slamming the front door behind him nanoseconds after he stepped over the threshold. "Are you fucking kidding me?" Stalking toward him, positively seething with murderous intent, I hissed out my next words between my teeth. "We were mated for all of two days before you ran away from me with your tail between your legs. So, no. There was no happiness."

Temporarily silent from the shock of my outburst, his body tensed, but his expression became even more resolved. "Korrina, you have to admit that it was a little bit of a shock for me to see my mate as a vampire."

Shrill, hysterical laughter bubbled out of me. "Would you like to know what else was a shock? You fucking … piece of shit … mother…" I trailed off, pinched the bridge of my nose, and counted to twenty. I couldn't believe he was making this about him. The nerve, the sheer arrogance of him! Taking a deep breath, I collected myself and continued my tirade in a calmer tone. "Oswin, do you have any idea what's it's like to wake up an entirely different person and then have to immediately go through

39

the pain of your mate leaving you during that life-changing crisis? You broke my heart in the worst possible way. I can't, won't forgive you for that."

"I'm truly sorry, darlin'. I have no excuse. I was a coward."

"Yeah, you were," I agreed. "So, don't expect anything but animosity from me."

Slowly, he stepped closer until he was in my line of vision. "Believe me, Korrina. I regretted it as soon as I left ... and not because you tried to bleed me dry. Darlin'—"

"Stop calling me that!" I shouted, pushing past him toward the door then yipping in surprise when the handsome male from next door opened it and poked his head in.

"Nobody shoot," he drawled. "I'm going to put her bags in the bedroom and get going."

I glared at Oswin and hissed, "How did you get my bags?"

Moving within whispering distance, Oswin said, "Easy, sugar. I didn't mess with your stuff. He's bringing in some things I thought would make you more comfortable here."

"I—" I stumbled over my next words. The closer Oswin came to me, the less sense my anger made. I couldn't seem to remember why I was mad, why I was so reluctant to forgive him. Hell, I couldn't seem to communicate at all. Him caring enough to buy things he thought would make me happier here was definitely giving me a case of the warm and fuzzies.

The good-looking wolf stepped inside, looking a bit skittish. "Should I come back another time?"

"It's fine," Oswin answered distractedly, not looking away from me. I knew why. He would be able to smell my arousal. Stupid, traitorous nymph hormones.

The male was all grace as he eased around us. "Be out of y'all's hair in a flash."

When he was out of earshot, Oswin fingered the front of my opened robe and murmured, "You look like a wet dream tonight."

My breath caught in my throat. Those words had a lot more of an effect than they should have. A lot more. They almost undid me. The impulse to give up the anger, to take him to bed and play out the thousands of fantasies I'd dreamed up since we'd been apart, would be so easy. And I wanted to … so, so badly.

"All right, I'm out of here," the blond wolf said. He was smiling when he came back into the room, but I knew he could sense, and possibly smell, the sexual tension between Oswin and I.

I turned my attention to him, welcoming the interruption, and stopped him with a trembling hand to his chest. "Who are you?"

The male flashed a sharp-toothed grin that spoke volumes. "The name's Klive, ma'am. Klive Williams."

Meeting his azure gaze head-on, I took a quick moment to size him up. It may have been almost four years since I was intimate with a shifter, but I remembered that spark, that energy. His curiosity was piqued by me being here. And he was turned on by my scent, just like his Alpha. "I'm Korrina Raines."

His eyes never left mine as he tipped an imaginary hat. "Pleasure."

Cocking my head, I narrowed my eyes. "Klive, are you a mated wolf?"

Surprised at the question, he blushed and studied the lines of the hardwood floor. "No, ma'am. I'm not."

I glided away from Oswin, closer to his body, an unmistakably seductive move that made him swallow hard. Tracing the white buttons of his shirt with the tips of my fingers, I purred, "I have to say I'm surprised about that, but I'm also glad. That makes things a lot easier for me."

His gaze focused on my mouth as I spoke. "What things?"

41

"What are you doing, Korrina?" Oswin asked, too late to stop the wheels I'd set into motion.

I didn't answer him. I just looked straight into the wolf's crystalline eyes and said, "Klive Williams, I choose you as my consort."

"What?" they yelled in unison.

Fed up with watching me all but seduce his pack-member in front of him, Oswin grabbed my hand, and none too gently forced me to face him. "I will do a lot of things to make you happy … a lot of things, Korrina, but I will not allow this. Not with him. Not with my second."

With pure, unadulterated hatred in my eyes, I spoke to my mate. "Oswin, you don't get to have a say in my choice. I know my rights."

"Look, I'm flattered," Klive said. "You're beautiful, like, crazy beautiful, and you seem really nice, but I don't think this is a good idea."

I gave him a sad little smile, straightening my nearly sheer nightgown and adjusting my robe. "It's kind of you to want to diffuse the situation, but, to be perfectly honest, you don't have a choice, either. Now, Klive, if you don't mind, I'd like to see where you live."

Klive looked to his Alpha with sheer panic in his eyes. Whether he was afraid of Oswin or me, I didn't know.

Oswin, who was livid and nearly shaking with rage, nodded his approval and glared at me. There was nothing else he could do. That, I was sure of. After all, he'd asked me to use this very law to choose Obsidian as my consort nearly four years ago. It was above reproach by any creature or law. The right was as old as time itself.

Smiling with the satisfaction of a battle won, I tugged Oswin's shell-shocked second past my mate with a look of determination in my eyes. I wouldn't let the bond and my nymph nature make me

Oswin's bitch, no pun intended. He would have to earn my love and trust the old-fashioned way, with hard work.

*** 

Outside, with my super sexy spoils of war, I had to ask myself … was I fucking insane? I was married! What the hell was I doing picking a stranger as a consort? Sure, he was pretty close to gorgeous. Well, gorgeous in a flannel shirt, worn-out jeans, and construction boots kind of way. But I didn't know him from Adam. What if he turned out to be a psycho, like another werewolf that shall remain nameless?

"That's me." Klive pointed next door. "It doesn't have much of a female's touch, though. Are you sure you wouldn't rather stay with your mate?"

"Don't call him that!" I snapped, following him to the next yard. "I have a mate, one that doesn't treat me like shit."

"I see." He was contemplative for a few seconds before saying, "Korrina, I want to apologize for the part I played in this. I heard what you said to him in there. I didn't know he left you because of your change."

I lifted a questioning brow. "I didn't know you were involved."

"Only in the sense that I went with him to Judge Manetas' office and encouraged him to do it," he said meekly. "But I promise you, if I had any idea of the circumstances, I wouldn't have."

I took his hand as we stepped onto the porch. "It's not your fault. You couldn't have known."

"Yeah, but that doesn't make me feel any less guilty … or freaked out," Klive admitted, looking everywhere except right at me. "Actually, everything is feeling a little surreal right now."

"Don't worry. I just can't be around him without wanting to throttle him yet. I'm hoping distance will make the heart grow fonder."

"Sometimes, I know the feeling." He shot me a grim smile as he unlocked his front door. "Do I need to invite you in or anything?"

"That's an old wives' tale," I said, smiling at the shake of his unsteady hand.

"Sorry." He made a 'ladies first' gesture. "I don't know much about vampires."

I shrugged and stepped inside. "There's not much you need to know. Just the blood and sunlight thing."

"About that, are you okay for blood?" he asked nervously. "I think Oswin has some at his house."

"You could just give me some of yours," I said, turning on the vampire-nymph charm. Facing him, I pressed him into the door he'd just closed behind us, fangs at the ready. "I could make it good for you, Klive. I could make it so damn good for you."

Momentarily speechless, he panted heavily and swallowed hard. "That may be the hottest thing I've ever witnessed."

I willed my fangs back into place and laughed, pleased at the change in the shy wolf. "Thanks. That's the nicest compliment I've gotten all week."

"Well, it's not every day that a female comes on to me—for my blood or otherwise," he said.

I moved in close enough to his body that I could hear the fast beat of his heart. "Why don't I believe that? You're strong, sexy, and your biceps are about to burst out of that flannel shirt. There's got to be someone here who appreciates all this hotness."

He blinked, and his blue eyes were replaced with ones of warm, burnished gold. "Korrina?"

"Yes?" I asked, enjoying his shudder when I rested my hand on his chest.

"You're a little dangerous to be around, aren't you?"

44

"Not as much as you think," I purred, trailing light fingers down his stomach, stopping short of the erection I knew waited there for me. "Like I said, consort or not, I won't drink your blood or try to have sex with you unless you ask for it. I know you're being forced into this consort thing. I won't force you into anything else." When he kept silent. I stepped away and changed the subject to a more comfortable one. "So, the creature really isn't into creature comforts, huh?"

"What do you mean?" He seemed confused by the sudden lack of contact.

I motioned around us. "I'd ask who your decorator is, but we both know you don't have one."

Klive saying that the house didn't have a female's touch was an understatement. It was clean, but that was all I could say about it. There was nothing on the walls, no rugs—really, no décor at all—only a couch and TV in the living room and a small table with two chairs in the adjoining kitchen. Spartan living had nothing on this guy.

"Uh..." He ran his hand through his hair, clearly embarrassed. "I work days on the construction crew and spend my evenings working around here or hunting with the pack. Between that and my sisters, there isn't much time for anything else."

"Like, putting up curtains?"

"Uh, yeah."

I sat on one end of the brown leather couch and patted the middle cushion. "Come sit next to me."

He hesitated, looking both intimidated and excited.

"I won't bite you," I told him.

"It's not you I'm worried about."

I smirked at the blatant innuendo. "Even so, get over here. Your Alpha female has questions."

Defeated, he sat on the couch, albeit all the way at the other end. "What do you want to know?"

"What's Oswin up to?" I blurted out.

"You don't waste any time, do you?"

"Not with things that are important to me, like, my freedom, my sanity, my way of life … you get the drift. So, spit it out."

"Korrina, I know you're looking for some big ulterior motive in this, but really, as far as I know, there isn't one. He wanted his mate back." Noticing my disbelieving face, he added, "I should tell you that he's spoken of little else for the past year and a half I've been in his pack."

I hadn't considered the possibility that Klive might not be from Oswin's original Thomasville pack. That opened up a whole other set of questions. "Okay, then. Tell me something I don't know. There's got to be something."

"There is." He sighed. "You've made the absolute worst choice in choosing a consort."

"Why? Do you like men?"

"No," he said, looking like he'd rather be anywhere else. "I'm inexperienced. There isn't much time for me to devote to a social life … assuming I ever find a mate my sisters approve of … or a mate, period."

"I know what it's like to have a lot of siblings. How many do you have?"

"Eight. All girls."

My mouth dropped open. "You poor thing."

"It's better now that they've stopped trying to paint my fingernails while I'm sleeping." He grinned and pulled a photo from his wallet. "This picture is from a few years ago, but they pretty much look the same today. That's Kalista on the left. Next to her is Karissa, and Keely and Kylie, who are twins. In the back, there's Koren, Keona, Kia, and Kiara."

"Your parents had a thing for K names, huh?"

"A little bit." He smiled at the picture of the blonde, grinning females. "They drive me crazy, but they're all I've got left. Our parents were killed around the time Oswin became Alpha of our pack."

Horrified, I gasped. "He didn't?"

"No. They lost their lives to the scum Oswin overthrew."

Moving closer, I put my hand on his much larger one. "I'm sorry."

He didn't look me in the eye. "It was a long time ago."

I took the hint and stood. "It's almost daybreak. I guess I need to get going."

"You can sleep here for the day if you want," he offered, looking hopeful.

"I can?" I asked, relieved I wouldn't have to go back to that lonely old house for a while. "Are you sure you don't mind?"

"Not at all. You can sleep in the bedroom with me. It already has blackout curtains."

Following him into a small, dark bedroom, I looked at the tiny twin bed and smiled. "That's going to be cozy."

"Too cozy?"

"No, I know how shifters like to touch skin, and I could use a little cuddle right about now, if that's okay with you."

Impulsively, he put his arms around me from the side and kissed my hair, lingering until his stomach growled. "I'll cuddle you all you want, Korrina," he said. "But it might have to wait until after breakfast. I'm starving."

I smiled and turned into his embrace to rest my head on his chest. "Thanks, Klive. I really needed this."

"This?"

"You. There's something so magnetic about you. You draw me in."

"Oh … uh, right. I'll be right back, okay?"

I lifted my head. "Where are you going?"

"To the communal cafeteria to get breakfast. Want me to bring something back for you? I don't think they're going to have blood, but I can definitely get a rare steak. Can you eat solid food?"

I cringed. "Could you make that steak well-done? Blood kind of freaks me out."

"Sure." He hesitated, looking amused. "I'll be back in a minute. Don't go anywhere, okay?"

I glanced out the unadorned living room window and saw lights flare to life in the house across the street. The wolves would be leaving for work soon, and I sure as hell wasn't ready to mingle yet. "Don't worry. I'm not going anywhere."

"Good. Because no one is going to believe I have a sexy vampire in my house without proof." He grabbed a clean flannel shirt from a stack of laundry on the dresser. "Here." He motioned to my skimpy sleepwear and blushed. "So, you can cover up."

"Thanks." I laughed as he gave me a little bow and walked out the door with a skip in his step. He was such a nice male, so sweet and friendly. I hadn't been lying to him in our embrace. He was exactly what I needed in my life right now.

# AT WIT'S END

## OSWIN

Hopeless. It was all hopeless. I couldn't keep Korrina under the same roof as me, no matter what tactic I employed. Nice guy, asshole—it didn't matter. She was going to hate my guts until I was my deathbed. How fitting.

I couldn't help but wonder how Obsidian managed to worm his way back into her good graces after they separated. How did he do it? Magic? Hypnotism? Sexual coercion?

Stopping still, I realized exactly what I needed to do. Digging around in my junk mail pile, I found the catalog I'd written Obsidian's cell number on and entered it on my own as fast as my fingers could dial, praying he was awake. I had no idea what time it was where he was at.

"What's wrong?" Obsidian asked in place of a greeting.

"What isn't," I retorted. "I don't know how you live with her. She's so clever; she's always one step ahead of me."

Obsidian laughed. "What has she done?"

"Laugh now," I told him gravely. "You won't be doing that when I tell you what she's done."

He yawned. "Spit it out, Oswin, so I can go back to sleep."

"Fine. Your wife is sleeping with another male."

There was silence for a few moments, then he asked, "Pardon?"

"She named Klive Williams, my second, her second."

"Her second what?"

"Consort! She's been hanging out at his house since she got here."

"She's already on the pack-lands?"

"Yes! Are you even listening?"

He sighed. "Is the male trustworthy?"

"I trust him implicitly," I said without hesitation. "I couldn't ask for a better second."

"Okay, so why are you calling me, Oswin?'

I couldn't believe how calm he'd asked the question. As if he couldn't care less that Korrina was shacking up with another male. "He's fucking her over there!" I yelled, hoping that raising my voice would somehow drive the point home.

Obsidian chuckled. "You can hear them having sex?"

"Well, no," I muttered. "But I can hear the laughing and playful giggling like they're in fucking stereo."

"Okay, so why are you calling me?" he asked again, this time sounding as if he'd already checked out of the conversation.

Irritated, I answered his question with a question. "Are you telling me you don't care that your wife has another male between her legs?"

"You mean, besides you?" he asked coolly.

I growled in frustration. "How the fuck are you so nonchalant about this? I thought you'd be on the next plane home!"

"Look, Oswin, she's a nymph, and I'm not naive. I knew, at some point, she was going to be sleeping with other males. You need to come to terms with that. If she fucks him, she fucks him. I just hope the male's ready for what that entails."

"You're not helping."

"I would, if I could, but I can't," he said in a genuine voice. "She's going to make you pay for what you did. I told you as much the last time I saw you. Take this as punishment number one for your misdeeds and move on. It's the only thing you can do."

"She's not like that," I argued. "She wouldn't do this on purpose."

"Are you so sure? She's hurt, and scared, and unwilling to be forced into forgiveness without hurting you back. You're just going to have to deal with it."

I scoffed. "Deal with it? That's your advice?"

"Oswin, it's ten in the morning here. I need to crash. If there's nothing else…"

"I don't know if I can do this, Obsidian."

Obsidian sighed again. "Brother, this is such a very small thing in the great scheme of things, a blip. Move on from this. Don't dwell on the hurt pride."

"I don't know if I can."

"I don't think you have a choice," he said, then the line went dead.

"Fuck!" I yelled, punching the wall and wincing when there turned out to be a stud behind the drywall. Obsidian was right. I had to deal with this shit. And deal with it, I would … if she ever gave me a chance.

# ANOTHER DAY, ANOTHER CONSORT
## KORRINA

By the time Klive stepped onto the front porch, balancing two heaping plates of food in his hands, I'd already completed my examination of his small house for serial killer evidence. I'd come up empty—thank God—and was feeling considerably better about staying with a perfect stranger that smelled like a wolf but, somehow, didn't seem like a wolf.

"Need a hand?" I asked him through the screen door, giggling at the perplexed look he was giving the handle.

He glanced at the pinkening sky on the horizon. "No. I don't want you to burn yourself."

"Hang on a sec." I opened the screen door wide and accepted one the plates, laughing at his horrified look. "Don't worry. I was never human, so I don't have an aversion to the sun."

"Give me a heart attack, why don't you!" he hissed, breathing heavily. "I instantly saw Oswin murdering me for letting you burn up."

"You worry too much," I said, sitting down at the small kitchen table to tuck into the giant rib-eye he'd brought me.

Klive sat across from me and stared at his own plate. A furrow marred his smooth forehead. "I want to keep you safe, Korrina."

"That's pretty chivalrous for someone who's being forced into housing a vampire."

He speared a piece of meat with his fork and chewed thoughtfully before he spoke. "I'm not being forced, but if you think it's more appropriate, I can try to stake you after breakfast."

"Funny," I said, rolling my eyes.

He got up and walked to the refrigerator. "Milk?"

"Yeah, but let me get it," I said, rushing to beat him to the fridge. "The least I can do is pour milk for you after you've put me up."

"Do you do toilets, too?"

"Don't push it," I said, smiling to myself. "Go sit yourself down before your food gets cold."

Klive grinned and held up his hands in mock surrender as he sidled past me. "Yes, Ma'am."

"That's more like it," I said, swatting his ass for good measure.

I expected him to laugh it off. We were both in a joking frame of mind. He didn't.

"I'm sorry," I told him quickly, sensing the change in his mood a millisecond before his body tensed and the gaze he shot me flickered from blue to gold and back.

His body was as lean and lithe as a cat as he gracefully stalked in my direction. "Korrina," he growled, his jaw clenched tight. He trapped my body against the counter with his and ran his nose along my jawline, inhaling my scent. "My scent on your body is driving me crazy."

He spoke with restraint, but I knew he had little of that to spare. He wanted me. And God help my soul, I wanted him, too. There was this strange pull in my heart when I gazed into his eyes. It was a sensation I had never felt before.

"Sorry," I said again, blushing when I realized I was staring at him with a mixture of awe and lust. "I forgot how close to your beast you guys can be."

He gave no audible response, but I was pretty sure he was counting down from a hundred as he sat. Eyebrows raised, I continued to pour the milk, deposited his glass next to his plate, and sat in my own seat without looking him in the eye.

"It's me that should be sorry," he said finally, his voice just above a whisper. "I shouldn't have said that to you."

"Klive, I've been presumptuous with you all morning. You have every right to tell me off, and as my consort, you have every right to have sex with me … if you want me."

"I want you," he said with zero hesitation.

I smiled at him and nearly melted when he smiled back with sharpened canines that gleamed a blueish-white in the fluorescent lights of the kitchen.

Suddenly nervous, he picked up his glass and drained it before saying, "You seem to know a lot about the pack's laws."

I nodded and blew out a shaky breath as the sexual tension evaporated from the room. "I do. I've been studying werewolf law pretty extensively since Oswin left me."

"That was probably a smart idea."

"It worked out pretty well for me today. I met a really nice wolf."

His smile faltered, but he recovered it quickly. "Tell me about yourself while we eat," he said.

I sat back and thought of a vague but plausible version of my life story. I wanted to trust Klive; he seemed like a nice guy, but there was always the possibility that he was related to one of the wolves in Oswin's last pack. Though it wasn't likely, he could be a grudge-holding relative of one of the wolves the trees killed in retaliation of my death. "Well, let's see, there's not much to tell. I'm from Alabama. I have twenty-seven siblings with another one on the way. Honestly, there's not much else to tell you."

"Did you say twenty-seven? Whoa. So, your parents, they're immortal?"

"Yes. My mom is seven-hundred and three on next Tuesday, and my dad is around one-hundred eighty years younger."

"Wow. Big age difference between them, huh?"

I swallowed a sip of milk and asked, "I don't think that means much when you're one of us, does it?"

He shrugged. "I guess not. What are they like?"

"Self-involved, stand-offish, but strangely over-protective? I really haven't spent enough time with them to give a more in-depth answer." I pursed my lips, trying in earnest to remember some kind of anecdote about my parents to tell Klive. Ultimately, I came up empty. "Nope. I got nothing. Tell me something about you. What do you do on the construction crew?"

"I'm foreman of Oswin's biggest crew."

"Then why aren't you at work? It's Thursday morning. Aren't you guys usually at the site at the crack of dawn?"

"Normally, yes, but when Oswin found out you were coming in last night. He asked me to hang around."

I cocked my head to the side in question. "Was he expecting trouble out of the wolves or me?

He shrugged again. "Take your pick."

Huffing, I said, "Well, that's both reassuring and insulting."

"Sorry," he said apologetically. "But, you know, safety first."

I gave him a sour look. "Thanks."

"You never told me what you do," he reminded me, steering us toward a much more amicable line of conversation. "Do you work? Volunteer?"

"I'm in the truffle business."

His eyebrows raised. "Truffles? As in, chocolate or mushrooms?"

"Truffles, as in, fungus. Don't look so surprised. I have sharp senses and can smell them for miles around. It's the perfect opportunity to make a ton of easy money."

He looked suitably impressed. "Are they around here, or do you have to travel to find them?"

"The most expensive varieties are in Europe, but there are some in the Pacific Northwest and the south that are becoming more popular by the day. My husband, Obsidian, does most of the traveling. He speaks French and Italian, so it's a big help."

"How long have you and Obsidian been married? Oswin keeps quiet on the details."

I refrained from rolling my eyes—barely. "Yeah, I bet he does. It's probably pretty embarrassing to admit he only mated me for his own selfish gain."

"What?" He made a "hurry up and spill" motion with his hands. "You have to give me more than that."

"Okay, but don't say I didn't warn you," I sang, laughing at his curious expression. "You might have to look at your precious Alpha in a different light after this."

He shook with suppressed laughter. "What I wouldn't give for Oswin to hear you call him precious."

"What I wouldn't give to be able to kick his precious ass," I retorted.

"This may be going out on a limb, but I'm sensing there's a lot more to the story that I don't know."

"You could say that," I told him. "Or you could say that four years ago, right around the time Oswin needed a mate to keep his Alpha status, he purposely started a semi-fake relationship with me to pull me away from Obsidian and avoid a challenge from his second."

His eyes widened in shock. "Well … fuck."

"Exactly!" I said exultantly, pointing my fork at him for emphasis. "So, you can see why I'm a little pissed to be back in Goshen."

"Yeah, I think I'm way ahead of you on that one. But what I don't get is why he did this to Obsidian? Couldn't he have found another female? One that wasn't already taken?"

"Well, technically, I wasn't taken. They kind of came along at the same time. But more importantly, I wasn't just any random female. A random female wouldn't have helped him in his revenge against Obsidian."

"Why did he want revenge? What did Obsidian do?"

"Obsidian married his sister in the nineteen-fifties."

His brows furrowed. "I still don't get it. Why would he be so upset about his sister marrying a vampire? It's been done before."

"Yeah, but his redneck, species-ist parents shunned her after she married him, and she grieved herself to death. I think when he saw the opportunity to avoid being challenged for Alpha and to get a dig in on Obsidian, he took it."

Klive looked contemplative while he chewed the last of his steak. I couldn't blame him; it was a lot to process. Finally, he swallowed and asked, "Do you think Oswin ever loved you?"

I sighed and dropped my eyes to my plate. "You know, I agonized over that for a long time after he left me. The bond was still so fresh, and I honestly did love him." I shrugged my shoulders. "But it's hard for him to love, I think. I'm not sure he really understands what it means to give everything you have to someone else."

Klive stood. "I've got to tell you, Korrina. I'm kind of seeing why you hate him so much. This whole thing is a shitload more complicated than he let on."

I stood and gathered our empty dishes. "Hence the consort thing with you, Klive. I don't want to be an imposition on you, but it's going to take a little time for me to get over this."

"You're not an imposition," he said. "I mean it. Stay here as long as you like. I'll deal with Oswin.

I set the dishes in the sink and put my arms around his middle. "Thank you."

He held me tight, resting his chin on the top of my head. "You gave him that scar, didn't you ... the one on his neck? He touches it when he thinks of you."

"I lost control," I told him. "Oswin hurt me so bad when he told me the truth. And I was new, brand new to being a vampire. My bloodlust got the better of me."

"Yeah," he agreed. "But I bet it felt pretty good when you did it."

I looked up at him and had to laugh at his expression. "It did have its moments."

"Wait a minute," he said, looking as if he'd had a revelation. "You said you were never human. What were ... are you?"

I pulled away and turned back to the sink. "A lady can have her secrets, can't she?"

"As long as a gentleman can," he answered enigmatically, handing me the glasses he'd gathered. He yawned and stretched against the door frame.

"You're tired," I told him. "Why don't you go lay down? I'll be in there in a minute. If you still want me there, that is."

He watched me wash our dishes for a moment then stepped forward to nuzzle my cheek with his. "I want you," he purred. "Don't doubt that. Good night, kitten."

"N-night," I stuttered, knowing damn well he would be able to scent my lust for him and would have noticed how my breath caught in anticipation when he caressed me so gently.

***

Klive had been thoughtful enough to leave an extra toothbrush and fresh washcloth in the bathroom for me before he went to bed. He was terribly sweet, a hazard of being a brother to so many females, I was sure. So far, there wasn't anything about him that wasn't one hundred percent adorable in my book. I had no doubt he would be a great mate for some lucky female one day. His sisters would have made sure of it.

A little shaky, I hung up the washcloth to dry and turned off the bathroom light, hesitating for a few minutes before I joined him in the bedroom. I was almost afraid to be alone with him in the bed. Being with him was already so comfortable. It wouldn't take much to take it to the next level. To be truthful, it wouldn't take much to fall in love with Oswin's second. There was something special about him. I just couldn't put my finger on what.

I found Klive on top of his duvet, curled up in the fetal position and fast asleep. I smiled at the boyish youth of his sleeping face. When he was alert, he was all sharp jawlines and sexy glares, but sleeping, he showed no signs of stress, no cares, as if he were young and untroubled, which had me wondering how old Klive really was. There was no way to gauge his age just by looking at him. Werewolves weren't immortal, but they lived for thousands of years. He could be thirty or nine-hundred and thirty and still look exactly the same. I secretly hoped he was around my age. With Oswin being however ancient he was and Obsidian getting close to one-hundred and forty years, it would be nice to find someone my age to talk to.

Before I resigned myself to whatever fate held for me, I grabbed an afghan blanket I spied at the bottom of the bed. It was cold for October, and sadly, high body temperature wasn't a trait I shared with the wolves. I would need the warmth. Unfolding the blanket, I spread half of it over his side and squealed in surprise when he reached up and pulled me under it with him.

"Mmmm … you smell good," he murmured sleepily.

I furrowed my brows, hoping he meant to devour me in a way I'd like. "I'm not sure how to take that statement from a strange wolf."

Maneuvering me into a spooning position, he yawned and buried his nose in my hair. "Take it as, Oswin is an idiot. Why would he give you up, sudden taste for human blood or not?"

I stayed quiet until I felt his breath even out with sleep. I didn't know how to answer that, either. How many thousands of times had I asked myself that very question?

A lot of thousands. That's how many.

# PACK MENTALITY ... OR JUST MENTAL
## KORRINA

I woke to the sound of many, many excited female voices. Sitting up, I pulled Klive's flannel shirt tight around me and shivered. He'd thrown another blanket over me sometime during the night, but it was still freezing without him curled around me to keep me warm.

Tip-toeing to the door, I peeked out of the crack to see the backs of four blonde women, sitting the couch and talking animatedly to Klive, who was looking both nervous and put out. Were these some of the sisters he'd told me about last night?

Klive glanced at the bedroom door and winced when he saw me there. I wasn't sure what that meant? I also wasn't sure if I should come out of his room with no pants on.

"Excuse me," he told the group, making his way toward me.

I stepped back to let him in, chewing on my lip. "Who are they?" I mouthed.

"Sisters," he whispered back.

I groaned. "I don't have any pants."

"I honestly don't think they'll care. They're just excited to meet you."

"How do they know I'm here?"

"I don't think there's a wolf in the pack that doesn't know you're here." He tapped his nose. "They can smell you."

"Oh, right ... my vampire stink."

"You do not stink. Yes, there is a hint of vampire, but underneath it, you smell like when it rains in the forest, fresh and piney."

I chuckled. "That's oddly specific."

He smiled. "You're an odd female."

"Thanks?"

He put an arm around me. "Come on, gorgeous. We have to get awkward introductions out of the way."

"They aren't going to wolf out because I slept in the same bed as their brother, are they?"

"I think it's way more likely you'll get your hair braided and be asked to go shopping."

"That, I can deal with. Lead the way."


Klive's sisters were, in a word, insane. They were loud, boisterous, and completely gung-ho on me becoming the vampire sister they'd never had before I even spoke. The collective squeal that ensued upon my arrival in the living room could have been heard from space.

"Oh, my gosh!" one of them yelled. "She's so pretty!"

"Pretty, hell. She's beautiful!" another one corrected. "Klive, you need to snap this one up. Anyone who can stand your snoring is a keeper."

"Come on, y'all," Klive reprimanded, though he was having a hard time keeping a straight face. "Give her some space. She's a little overwhelmed." He rubbed the circulation back into his arm where I'd been clinging him and whispered, "You've got quite the grip."

"Sorry, Klive."

"Awwwww..." they chorused.

He shook his head. "Y'all don't embarrass me too much, okay?"

"Yeah, right," the tallest of the group said, before grabbing my hand and dragging me to the couch. "Girl, you have to tell us about yourself. All we know is that you're a vampire and that you have great taste in men."

I looked pleadingly at Klive.

He shrugged. "Sorry, you're on your own. I have to go next door to talk to Oswin about work … and other more uncomfortable things."

"Coward," I mouthed.

"Yep. Sorry 'bout that, too. But, I know them. They just do pretty much whatever they want, regardless of what I say."

His sisters all nodded in agreement.

"All right, what do you guys want to know?" I asked as I watched Klive skulk out the door.

"Well, first things first, where did you meet our brother?" the sister in red asked.

"We met at Oswin's house."

"And how do you know Oswin?" another sister asked.

I cringed, hoping they wouldn't hate me. "I'm his mate?"

"WHAT?" they screeched in unison.

"I mated Oswin a few years ago," I said, sighing heavily. "We just … I guess you could call it … reconciled? I mean, I wouldn't. On account that he's pretty much the biggest douche I know."

The tall sister clapped her hands in joy, making me jump. "Oh, this is going to be good."

"It might be," I told her. "If you like hearing disparaging comments about your Alpha."

She looked at her sister's eager faces. "Looks like we're in luck!"

I grinned. "Okay, I'll give you all the sordid details, but first, tell me your names, so I can stop referring to you as 'red shirt', 'blue shirt', and 'the tall one' in my head."

They giggled.

"I'm the oldest, Koren," said the blue-shirted sister. "The excited one over there is Kalista. The red shirt is Keely and Kylie here is her twin sister. There are four more of us, Kia, Keona, Karissa, and Kiara, but they're at work."

"It's nice to meet you all."

Kylie waved her hand. "Yeah, yeah. Us, too. Now get on with the story."

I laughed. "Let's see. How about I start at the beginning? You really have to hear the whole story to understand my hatred for Oswin."

"Sounds good to me," Kalista said.

"Well, it all started with me meeting Oswin a few years ago when I moved into the house next door to the pack-lands. He pursued me, mated me under false pretenses, and then totally screwed me over once I became a vampire."

Koren raised her brows. "What kind of false pretenses?"

"Oh, nothing major. His ex-pack-member killed a human to frame the vampire that was renting me the house, and to save me from going down with him, Oswin offered diplomatic immunity via a hasty mating. I thought, at the time, he was doing me a favor. But what I didn't know was that he needed to mate someone to keep his status as Alpha … and to even the score with the vampire, who was his ex-brother-in-law."

"Whoa," Keely said. "I mean, I knew he had a mate; Klive mentioned it a couple times. But I don't think even he knew about all that! How did Oswin screw you over once you turned?"

"He split."

"Split?" Kylie asked, looking genuinely confused. "Werewolves don't leave their mates—ever."

I smiled bitterly as I thought of Oswin's reaction to my turning. "Well, your pack-master did. He dropped me like a hot potato and ran away with his tail between his legs ... until I caught him."

Kalista guffawed. "Please, please tell me you handed his ass to him."

"I guess you could say that. I did snatch his retreating ass out of his truck and try to drain him dry."

"Holy shit!" Koren exclaimed. "I'd say that counts!"

I pursed my lips. "I was so new. Like, ten minutes new. I didn't know what I was doing. Thank God, Obsidian was there to stop me."

"Is Obsidian the homeowner?" Kylie asked.

"Yes, and my husband under human law. We married a little while back and just moved to Goshen from the vampire community in Everlast, Virginia at Oswin's request."

Kylie shook her head. "This is better than a soap opera!"

I grimaced. "Not from where I'm sitting."

"So, how did a vampire with a mate and a husband get mixed up with our brother?" Keely asked.

"I named him my consort when I met him last night."

"Way to stick the knife in!" Kalista exclaimed. "I'll bet Oswin was livid!"

"Oh, he was really pissed, but I just couldn't give in to our bond so easily after what he did. He hasn't been punished long enough. Not by a long shot. And when I saw Klive, I thought, 'Why not?'. He's a nice, sweet guy, and if he wants to actually go through with everything the consort thing entails, it wouldn't be such a chore for me. He is beautiful."

Koren leaned back into the cushion of the couch. "Wow. And gross."

I sighed. "Yeah. I hated to involve Klive in this craziness, but what's done is done now. I hope you guys aren't too mad about it."

"Mad? I'm ecstatic. Klive needs a female in his life. I never thought it would be the Alpha female of my wolf pack, but whatever." She shrugged. "A lady friend is a lady friend."

I glanced around at Klive's sisters. "I'm really glad you're okay with this."

Keely grinned. "I'm super okay with it. Koren is right. Klive needs a lady in his life, even if it's only for a short time. Is it only going to be for a short time?"

"I honestly don't have an answer to that. I thought so, but there's something about him that draws me in, some kind of connection between us. It's weird."

"Maybe you're kismet?" Kylie asked. "The fates work in mysterious ways. Just ask the seer of the pack. She talks about that all the time."

"You have a seer? Is she a wolf?"

"Yep. Thusnelda is ancient. She's been in the pack for thousands of years. Talking to her is a trip. She knows A LOT."

I sat back, thinking Kylie's words over. What if Klive and I were kismet? What did that mean for Oswin and me? Hell, what did that mean for Obsidian and me?

"Oops. I think we broke her, ladies," Kalista said, laughing.

"No," I assured her. "I'm just thinking about this kismet thing. With the way my life has gone over the past few years, it wouldn't surprise me if Kylie were right."

"Well," Kylie said. "There's only one way to find out."

"You mean ask the seer?" I asked warily.

"Yes, ma'am!"

"I don't know if I'm ready for that. And I'd probably need pants, and I don't have any here."

"You don't have pants here?" Keely asked. "Never mind. I don't want to know."

They all laughed until they saw Klive step back onto the porch.

"He's baaaack!" Koren singsonged.

"Yeah, but I'm not sure if it's safe to enter," Klive said through the screen door. "The last time I heard all of you laughing like that, I woke up with fake eyelashes."

Kalista stood up. "Come on, girls. Think there's a certain seer we need to see."

"Ooohhh, yes!" Koren said excitedly. "Gotta go, bro. See you guys later!"

"Don't leave without me!" Kylie said, dragging her twin behind her. "See ya, Korrina!"

"Bye!" I called after them.

Klive looked at me with a confused expression. "What just happened?"

I stood and wrapped my arms around him, melting into the warmth of his broad flannel-covered chest. "I couldn't explain it even if I wanted to."

# A TRULY EPIC PACK MEETING
## OSWIN

Klive ushered Korrina up the steps of the community center seconds before the full moon meeting was about to start. She didn't say anything to me as she passed by, only continued her one-woman mission to cause actual harm by staring at me with a glare that had the heat of a thousand suns. It had been two days since she'd arrived, and this was the first I'd seen of her, though I'd heard she'd made a few appearances on the pack-lands and at the community center. I had no idea if she'd even been home yet. I wasn't sure I wanted to know.

As I watched them together, it was evident that Klive had been blessed with the magic of the divine. He had to be. Nothing short of a minor miracle would have gotten her to honor my request to show up. She was still so damn angry. Not with Klive, of course. She was eating right out of the male's hand, laughing, and making cow eyes like someone at the beginning of a relationship. Exactly like she used to do with me.

In an effort to be civil, I asked, "Are you ready to meet the pack, Korrina?" when I caught up to them.

Total silence.

"Right," I muttered, not about to comment on it. "Follow me. Let's not keep them waiting." I led her up the aisle to the front of the fifty or so folding chairs and waited on the pack to settle.

"Am I going to have to say my name and admit that I'm a sexaholic?" Korrina asked me in a whisper, her tone mocking.

I knew she was trying to rile me up, but I laughed anyway. I couldn't help but feel giddy that she'd said actual words to me, and the room did look like we were about to discuss a twelve-step program. "You don't have to say a thing unless you want to," I told her, then raised my arms to quiet the crowd. "Thanks, everyone, for coming. As you can see, we have a guest on the pack-lands tonight."

"See, hell!" my secretary, Tabitha, yelled. "We've all heard about Klive's new girlfriend. "I had to pay Kia twenty bucks when I bet her she was imaginary!"

Klive pulled his baseball cap down over his eyes and sank lower in his chair. Poor guy. Any lower and he'd be sitting on the floor.

Smiling a little, I shook my head. It was weird, but even after all I had to endure over the past couple of days, I felt terrible for the guy. He was such an innocent male, and they would tease him mercilessly for this over the next few weeks ... or months. Once they found out he was the Alpha's consort, too, Klive might want to think about moving out of the state ... or the stratosphere. It was going to be sheer hell.

"That's enough," I scolded. "Give it a rest, and please join me in making my mate, Korrina Raines, feel at home here." Ignoring the dead silence, which was unheard of in any group of three or more werewolves, I plowed on. "I'm going to ask that you do not bombard her with questions tonight. Everyone will have plenty of time to get to know her."

"Some of us already have, right, Klive?" Kalista asked, barely holding it together. Apparently, his sisters were well aware of the situation.

"No more of that," I warned. "Respect your Alpha's decision to choose a consort."

"Consort?" Hayden asked. He was barely of age. It was doubtful he and many of the others had ever heard the word uttered before. The law was antiquated and wasn't well tolerated in modern packs without a damn good reason.

"Choosing a consort is the right of any Alpha female or male," I clarified. "Yes, it was originally enacted to prevent the extinction of our species, but it can be used for any reason deemed necessary ... or unnecessary, by either Alpha. That said, I'm fine with her

69

choice, which means you will be fine with it, or you can answer to me. While on the pack-lands, my mate should feel free to mate with either of her two consorts at her own discretion."

"Two?" Brent asked, looking impressed. "What? One shackle isn't enough?"

"You do realize I can beat you within an inch of your life, don't you?" Candace asked, before smacking the back of her mate's head.

I tamped down the irritation their levity brought on. I had to keep my head, though I didn't think my ego had ever taken a more severe beating. "All right, guys, let's get this done before Candace makes her pups wards of the state." When they were mostly settled, I added, "Now, as far as Korrina's other consort goes, he'll also be spending time on the pack-lands."

"Is he from another wolf pack," Hayden asked.

"No, Obsidian Raines is a vampire."

I'd expected the stunned silence of the mate bombshell, but the exact opposite happened. Several wolves shot up from their seats in protest, and the room erupted into chaos.

Yelling over the excited and angry voices in the crowd, I said, "I know that some of you may take issue with having a vampire on the pack-lands, but I warn you, the prejudices of your prior pack will not be tolerated. All preternatural creatures need to stick together. I shouldn't have to remind you how outnumbered we are by the humans."

"Vampires are in no danger of dying out," Scott retorted, rolling eyes that had went wolf at the mention of vampires. "It's ridiculously easy to make a human a vampire."

"Vampires like Obsidian are. He's a true vampire, born not turned."

Surprised whispers broke out among the crowd.

"He's also a long-time member of my pack," I continued. "He has had a place here since the night he married my sister in nineteen fifty-five. That is longer than almost everyone here has been alive. Do not think that I do not value him because he is a different species; I do. I consider him to be my brother." I eyeballed everyone in the room, showing them that I meant business. "Continuing on that subject, your Alpha female is also a vampire, albeit only half. The same rules apply, though I will say that Korrina needs no help defending herself. Mess with her at your own peril. Now does anyone have any questions?"

Several hands shot up.

"Tarin?" I called, pointing in her direction.

The tall, brunette she-wolf stood up and gave us a smile and a silly little curtsy. "Pardon me, if it's rude, but is it true your mate is also a nymph?"

I didn't have to answer the question. Korrina did … in a sense. As soon as the question fell from Tarin's lips, the trees around the building spoke for her, their voices ethereal and lilting.

"Korrina is a child of nature."

The crowd gasped and stared at their Alpha female. I was staring at her, too. Out of fear or awe, I wasn't sure. "Well, I guess that answers that," I told the crowd, facing them again. "Anyone else?"

No one said a word. They only stared.

"All right, if there are no more questions, I'll excuse Korrina. I'm sure she has things she'd like to do tonight."

No sooner than the words were expressed, Korrina walked toward the exit, an apologetic but bemused Klive following her to the double doors.

"Wait just a moment, you two," a withered, raspy voice said from the middle of the crowd.

Klive and Korrina jerked their heads toward the voice. "Thusnelda," Klive said solemnly, giving a slight bow as he greeted the frail werewolf elder. He knew she didn't make herself known to just anyone.

"That's enough of that formal stuff, Klive," Thusnelda admonished as she ambled closer. "You couldn't know this, but I've waited over a thousand years to say what I'm going to tell you tonight." She gave Korrina a bright grin. "But before I get to that, I want to say that Oswin gets too big for his britches sometimes. I think you're right to do what you're doing to him, Korrina. He needs to be put in his place.

"Thanks," she said, smiling at the crowd's snickers then arching an 'I told you so' brow at me.

Thusnelda grinned again. "You're most welcome, honey. But I'm not here to talk about the Alpha. No, I came here to talk about the two of you."

Korrina shot Klive a questioning look. He shrugged.

I held my breath as Thusnelda stared into the distance with grey, unseeing eyes. "I saw you, Korrina," she said, gripping her hand. "In my dreams, I saw you coming for Klive. He's in your future, you know. Surely, you feel it."

"I feel … something," she said in a small voice, unable to look away from Klive's exalted face. "But what can I do about it? I love my husband … and my mate."

Every bit of air whooshed out of my lungs when I heard her whisper those three magical words. Korrina loved me. She still loved me. I felt my whole body loosen with relief as I strained to catch every single syllable the old wolf was saying.

"Korrina, we all make sacrifices for the things we love," she told her. "You'll do that for Klive and Obsidian, and Oswin will do that for you." She tapped her head. "I've seen it. Your future is actually one of my more exciting visions.

Klive finally broke eye contact with Korrina to look at the prophetess. "You've seen our future?"

She nodded and closed her eyes. "Two beautiful creatures, one light and dual-natured, one dark with the magical blood of the demigod, Dionysus, will be born under the same moon. Their union will catapult the vampires and weres into peace, once and for all."

"Whoa," Kia said. She was hanging on every word.

"Just you wait, there's more," Thusnelda told her, obviously as pleased as punch to tell everyone what she'd known for ages. "Where was I? Oh, I've got it. And after the great wolf, Oswin, departs from the Earthly plane, their grandchild will rule for a thousand years. He will be a well-loved Alpha and king of vampires." She opened her eyes and smiled. "That's all I can see before my own life ends."

"Our grandchild?" Korrina asked.

Her words came out like a question, but it was more of a statement of disbelief. I could relate. I was stunned by the news. My mate pregnant with another shifter's young? It was unfathomable, unimaginable.

Thoughtful, Thusnelda answered, "Yes, the son of your second son, I believe."

"We'll have more than one child?" Klive asked excitedly. He was obviously about to burst with joy at the news of him being a father.

"Yes, Korrina will bear three children. All will be blessed with the talents of their fathers."

Disappointment marred Klive's happy expression. "What does that mean?"

"It means that she will bear triplets that will share all four of their parent's DNA."

He looked stricken. "We'll all be their father?"

"Don't worry," Thusnelda told him. "All of Korrina's sons will love you as a father. In fact, they will spend a great deal of their time with you. And you will see them all grow to have their own grandchildren. You are in no way deprived of your chance of having a family or your 'own' child. You will be beloved by all that are around you."

Sheepish, he glanced away from my mate and asked, "Will Korrina be one of those around me?"

She grimaced. "Rest assured, Korrina will worship you until the end of your days."

It seemed unreal, but even as Thusnelda said the words, I could feel our fates cement themselves together. Somehow, hearing her words made it all real, made it a reality, whereas before, children were only a far-fetched dream.

"Thank you, Thusnelda," Klive said, bowing in the traditional way. "I can't tell you what this means to me."

"You're welcome," she said seriously. "But you listen here. You're going to need to support your mate. Your life will be an easy road compared to hers."

"Yes, ma'am."

With her prediction spoken, Thusnelda sprinted back to her seat faster than I thought possible for a wolf at her age and grinned goofily at the wolves staring openmouthed at her. "What?"

Korrina blushed as our eyes met. I wanted so much to tell her that everything was going to be all right, to hold her, to show her how much I wanted what was predicted, no matter how it came about, but I had to content myself with the knowledge that she would one day forgive me. For now, that would have to be enough.

I held up a finger to silence the pack for a minute after Klive and Korrina left the room. When I was sure they were out of earshot, I grabbed a chair and sat down backward to speak frankly to the pack. I decided, with this pack, I would be open and forthcoming in a bid to get them to behave the same way. Some would call that leading by example, but frankly, it was a desperate attempt to keep the tree's massacre of the Thomasville wolves from happening again. I had to make sure this pack didn't repeat my last pack's mistakes. If not for me, for my sons.

"What the hell just happened?" Peter asked.

I shook my head. "I don't know. This is the first I've heard of it, too. But, guys, I want you to put all that prophecy business aside for a second. I have something serious I need to discuss." When I had the room's full attention, I said, "I'm sure it's obvious to you that Korrina doesn't want to be here."

"Yeah, no kidding," Keona said sarcastically.

I pursed my lips. "Don't blame her for the coldness she showed today, Keona. That's all my fault. No one in her position would want to be here after what I did to her."

"What did you do?" Brent asked.

"I abandoned her on her deathbed, right after her change, a change caused by a member of my own pack." Gasps and angry glances replaced the whispers of speculation. Now that they knew why Korrina was so reluctant to be civil, I doubted anyone blamed her for the unfriendly way she'd acted. Anyone with two brain cells to rub together could see that her actions were aimed directly at me and no one else. "I know what I did was terrible," I continued. "You don't know how much I know that. I should have been a decent male and thanked the Lord my brother-in-law was able to save her life with vampirism." I sighed. "I should've accepted her fate and mine."

Tabitha tsked. "For shame, Oswin."

I nodded, my eyes cast down. "Tab, I am so ashamed. I'm ashamed of what I thought, what I did, and I know I don't deserve her forgiveness; I never will. But I can't live without her. That's why I'm asking for your help in making her feel at home here."

Kalista stood up, hands on hips. "You're a fucking asshole, Oswin."

"You can say that again," Keona said, snickering at my discomfort.

"I'm not disputing that, you two, but I am trying to change that. Do you think you can help me?"

"I'm not sure there's any helping you," Keona's slightly older sister, Karissa, told me. "Who the hell leaves their mate on her deathbed?"

"Especially one that looks like that," her mate, Peter, commented, wriggling his eyebrows.

"Is anyone taking this seriously?" I asked. "I need a game plan."

"She's not a pick-up game after dinner," Koren reprimanded. "Vampire-nymph or not, she's still a lady."

I hung my head. "I am such a schmuck."

"Yep," Koren said. "And you're going to have to grovel to get back in her good graces."

"And beg," Kylie added.

Thusnelda stood, her sharp eyes piercing through me like a laser beam. "Oswin, you make this right. You've hurt that female something awful. You make it right, or I'll beat the tar out of you. Your choice."

I smiled at the cantankerous she-wolf. "Nelda, I'm going to try as hard as I can. Give me some time before you skin me alive."

"I'll give you a week."

"Fair enough."

Peter whistled low. "This is going to be the longest week of your life."

# WELCOME TO PANIC CITY

## KORRINA

From the community center, I ran straight toward the woods. The need to be away from Oswin and Thusnelda's prophecy was so overwhelming, I couldn't breathe.

But I knew what I needed to do. There was really only one thing that soothed me when I was upset—the trees. When it comes to needing to be cheered up, nothing beat the rush of healing energy nymphs receive from being in the forest. Touching a tree or bush gave us a sense of peace, of calm. Calm was definitely what I needed at the moment.

The closest tree was a tall pine that welcomed me with excitement. I trailed my hand across the trunk and smiled at the tingle of life it gave me in return. We didn't steal the tree's energy, per se. It was sort of a recycling process. We took their vitality and pushed it back into them with a boost of magic. As strange as it sounded, the act benefited us both. The trees were catapulted into a renewal cycle that extended their longevity, and we were granted the right to use nature as we see fit, feel grounded, and are further rewarded with a soothed soul and clear mind.

The trees also gave fantastic advice. Being around humans for so many thousands of years, seeing the misery they brought on themselves, they picked up a trick or two, and they sure weren't shy about sharing those tricks. As much as I hated to depend on someone else, I had to admit, having an objective party to bear witness to your problems and give unbiased advice was a godsend when your emotions are running the show instead of your common sense.

"Hello," I said to the stand of trees around me, laying my hands on another healthy pine.

*"Hello, young one,"* it said in answer.

"You're one to talk!" I scolded. "What are you, forty, max? You can't be more than ten years older than me."

Pine straw rained down as the tree shook with silent giggles.

"Hey!" I screeched, dodging a pine cone. "That was too close!"

Two more cones fell before a much more mature tree interrupted the pine's playtime. *"Korrina,"* it murmured. *"You have returned to our grove. We welcome you home."*

"Thank you. It's good to be back," I lied.

*"Truly?"*

"No," I admitted, my eyes tearing up. "I lied. I'm sorry."

*"Speak your mind, little one. What troubles you?"*

"I don't know what I'm doing here. I feel like my life is spiraling out of control."

*"You are here because the wolf needed his mate. He is very lonely. He pines."*

I rolled my eyes at the obvious pun. "That coward made his choice when he ran away from me."

*"Coward? Your mate is admired across many miles. So much hatred was eliminated by his actions, so many innocents spared. He is nothing short of a hero to us all."*

"All that may be, but that doesn't change the fact that I was abandoned by him."

*"Korrina,"* a magnolia admonished. *"Forgive him. Have you never made a mistake?"*

I cringed inwardly at the thought of how I had betrayed Obsidian's trust by claiming another consort so soon after my arrival. But that emotion was quickly replaced by another … anger. The trees were right. I would have to forgive Oswin … and have his pups. That really, really pissed me off. Fury roiled through me so fast and pure, I had to clench my teeth against it. I couldn't believe that after everything he did to me, I had to be the one to make amends. That I had to be the bigger man … woman … nymph … whatever.

With a grimace, I snapped my head up and scanned the moonlit meadow for movement when I heard the loud crunch of dry leaves in the distance. Someone was coming. And with the way they were carelessly tromping through the woods, I doubted it was Klive. He could've snuck up on me without me ever knowing about it. This visitor was not pack, or if they were, they were purposely making a ton of noise to ensure that I was presentable by the time they got here. With the wolves' superior hearing, they might have heard my distraught conversation with the trees.

I wiped the angry tears from my eyes with a sleeve and tried to pull it together. I could do this. I could pretend everything in my world was normal. I could pretend I didn't love Oswin. I could pretend I wasn't foretold to be the mother to a few vampire-wolves. I could do all that.

No. No, I couldn't. My life was anything but ordinary. I couldn't imagine my problems away. Maybe, one. Two tops. But not all of them.

"Who's there?" I called to the visitor, tired of waiting for them to show. There was no answer. I walked toward the noise's point of origin and tensed, ready to take on whoever was out there should I need to. "I know you're there," I yelled. "I can sense you."

"Can you?" a smooth, accented voice asked.

My breath caught in my throat. The voice sounded like Agapios'. But he couldn't be here. I was banished to Goshen for five years for my role in our tryst behind the Meadowbrook Starbucks. There was no way he could be here without breaking the conditions of his punishment. If my calculations were correct, and Solon continued to practice the strict adherence to the law he always did, Agapios should have at least another year before his exile was over. He didn't have an Alpha wolf to give him diplomatic immunity like I did.

Once the initial shock wore off and I found my voice, I hissed, "What are you doing here?"

"I'm checking on you," Klive said, coming into view on my left.

"Were you just over there?" I asked, pointing into the distance on my other side.

"No, I went to the house after we left the meeting to give you a minute alone."

Nervous now, I whispered, "There's someone out here."

His amused demeanor changed to one of lethal concentration. He inhaled deeply through his nose, scenting the air. "What is that? I don't recognize the smell."

"Satyr."

His eyebrows rose. "Those are real?"

"Yeah, and I have a history with this one. I'll have to call my Uncle Solon when I get back to your house. He'll know what's up."

"Should I alert Oswin?"

"I'm not sure. It may be nothing. Agapios probably wants to talk to me. Being surrounded by shifters can't make that an easy process."

He took another deep breath and scanned the area. "He's gone."

"Good."

"So," he said. "That was pretty interesting back there."

Sinking down to sit on the roots of an old sweet gum tree, I sighed and stared down at the ground in front of me. "Which part, the prophecy or the trees?"

"Let's start with the trees," he said, smiling at me with pure adoration.

"I don't know why I did that."

"I do." He settled cross-legged in front of me, his blue eyes twinkling with the same mischief I usually found there.

"You do?"

"Yeah. Animals tend to make themselves seem bigger and scarier than they normally are when they're cornered. Apparently, nymphs do, too." He took my hand and pressed his lips to my knuckles. "You had every right to be nervous, you know, especially after what I now know happened in Thomasville. You just wanted everyone to know that you could still defend yourself. That's all." He winked and lowered his voice. "Mission accomplished, by the way."

"Thanks, I guess." I studied his face, wondering what the combination of his and Oswin's fair features and Obsidian's dark ones would look like on our children. There was no doubt they'd be handsome. That was a given, no matter which father they favored. They were all so good-looking in their own way. "So, do you think there's any chance she's wrong?"

He gave me an encouraging half smile. "Nope. Her predictions are never wrong. She was the seer in my last pack."

"Then I'm going to be a mother," I said absently. "A mother to were-vampire nymphs."

"There's something you don't hear—ever."

I laughed. "That's because it's crazy."

"Crazy good," Klive said, grinning widely. "I'm going to have babies."

I rolled my eyes. "I'm glad someone is excited about this."

"Excited? I'm ecstatic! She said our children would bring the weres and vampires together. What could be better than that?"

"Yeah, that part is great, but forgive me if I'm a little more concerned with the part where she said you'd have it easier than me. Is she referring to me having to push out three younglings or something else? And what did she mean by we were born under the same moon?"

He smiled. "Females have been pushing those out since the beginning of time."

"Easy for you to say," I muttered.

"I guess that's true," he agreed, his expression contrite. "I'm sorry."

I shook my head. "No, I'm sorry. I'm ruining this for you."

Leaning forward, he slipped his arms around me. "You couldn't possibly, Korrina. Nothing could."

Resting my head on his shoulder, I buried my face into his neck. It felt nice to be close to Klive like this, so right. The smell of his hair, the smooth tan skin under my lips, the lean muscle of his chest under my palms … it all made me forget everything else. I just wanted to immerse myself in his very presence and let his soothing warmth wash over me.

"Korrina?" Klive asked, his voice little more than a growl.

I pulled away and met Klive's eyes. They were no longer human. "Yes?"

He leaned forward and brushed his lips against mine, lingering for a moment. "What is it about you?"

"Hmmm?" I asked. I was so lost in his gold gaze; I couldn't think beyond my need for him. Nothing made sense right now but him and the connection between us.

His eyes flickered back to blue as he mumbled, "Born under the same moon."

"Huh?"

Pulling away, he asked, "How old are you, Korrina?"

"Thirty-one. Why?"

His eyebrows shot up. "And on what day were you born?"

"August twelfth."

"That's it," he nearly shouted, standing up suddenly. "That's what she meant."

"What's it?" I asked, holding up my hand for help.

He pulled me to my feet. "We were born on the same day. And I'd bet anything we were born at the same time, too."

"What time were you born?"

"9:15 PM."

My eyes widened. "Same."

"Do you think…" he trailed off, looking embarrassed.

"That we're soulmates?" I asked.

He nodded. "Yeah."

I raised my hand to his cheek. "I think so, yes."

***

Klive invited me out the next night. I accepted the invitation with a grateful smile and a precariously fragile state of mind. Last night had been the hardest night of my short life. Not only did I have to come to terms with the unexpected news of the triplets, a new soul-mate, and my begrudging acceptance of Oswin, I still hadn't heard from Obsidian in Italy. He never called as he promised he would, and all of my increasingly desperate calls went straight to voicemail, prompting me to think the worst. Either he was dead, or I was dead to him.

Determined not to let my fears get the better of me, I met Klive in his driveway promptly at eight o'clock, wearing a low-cut little black dress that I'd been saving for a special occasion … any special occasion.

Klive opened the passenger side door and helped me up into his truck. "You look amazing," he said reverently.

"Thanks," I said, my cheeks pinkening with a blush. When he climbed into the cab next to me, I added, "You look pretty good yourself, you know."

"Yeah, I know. That's a given," he told me with a wink.

"Egotistical much?" I asked.

He snickered. "Oh, come on. I see those longing glances you're throwing my way. Is it the tight jeans or the eyes? Ladies love blue eyes."

I rolled my own bright green ones. "You need professional help."

"Yeah, I've heard that before." He grinned and looked behind him to pull out of the driveway. "So, how was work today?"

"Meh," I said. "Same old, same old. Paperwork and phone calls."

"I can relate to that. Well, the same old, same old thing, anyway." He backed out of the driveway and drove toward the main road. At the stop sign, he said, "That settles it. We're young, reasonably attractive, and supernatural. We're going to paint the town tonight."

"Did you just say, 'paint the town'?" I asked, my eyes wide with amusement. I was trying hard not to laugh.

"No comment."

A few minutes passed before either one of us said anything. He let me go first. Apparently, he was afraid he wouldn't be able to string a sentence together that wasn't circa nineteen-fifty.

"So, where will tonight's painting take place?"

He wriggled his eyebrows. "Somewhere worthy of that sexy dress."

I smiled in the darkness. "Where's that?"

"You'll see," he said, giving me a Cheshire Cat grin.

"I don't know if I like this 'mysterious Klive'," I said, aiming a sour look at him.

He grinned at my frustration. "How's this? You'll never guess where I'm taking you, not in a million years. You're welcome to try, though," he added, just to complete my torture.

I squinted at him. "Am I going to have to kick your ass before the night is over?"

Flippant, he grinned and drawled, "Don't know. I'm not a mind-reader."

I smacked his thigh with my open hand. "So what you're saying is that you didn't see that coming?"

"Ow!" He rubbed his leg to get the blood circulating again. "Don't forget about your vampire super strength, you vicious thing. That hurt!"

"Sorry," I told him, my voice placid and not at all sorry. "I forgot who I was with. I'm not used to hanging around with werewolves who have the constitution of a little old lady."

"Shut it, you," he griped, trying to hold back the smile tugging at the corners of my mouth. "Oswin was right. You can be a real handful."

***

Klive and I shared stories of our many siblings on the hour-long drive, but even with that much time to devote to the subject, we still only managed to talk about twenty of the thirty-six. I wasn't surprised. The description our families could be covered in one word, and that word was massive.

"Okay," he said. "We're almost there. I want you to try to contain your excitement when you see where we're going."

"With all this buildup, I'm going to be disappointed if we're not going to Disney World."

"Well, since we're going in the opposite direction and it hasn't been eleven hours, I'm going to go ahead and prepare you for imminent disappointment."

I sighed. "I never get to have any fun."

"Yeah, you're right, Cinderella. Say, shouldn't you be home scrubbing a hearth or something?"

"Shut your mou—" I broke off, my eyes darting toward a rundown bar's parking lot. "Is that a dead deer?"

He slowed down to turn into the bar's driveway and parked next to the old pickup truck with the deer. "Yep. Is that going to be a problem?"

I stared at him. "Where the hell are we, Klive?"

"Alabama?" he asked, grinning as he answered my question with one of his own.

"The bar, asshole."

He snickered. "Oh, that. Korrina, welcome to Dancing Bob's Bar and Grill. It's full of rednecks, watered down beer, and old country on the jukebox, but it has the best damn chicken strips this side of the Mississippi. I thought you looked like the kind of female that could appreciate a good chicken strip."

The second he hinted at fried chicken, my smile lit up the truck up like the sun coming out on a rainy day. He was right. I did appreciate a good chicken strip. "I think I love you," I said, ignoring the peeling paint and ancient Pabst Blue Ribbon sign. I knew the look of a building had little to do with good food in these parts.

"Chicken makes you radiant," he muttered in surprise.

I opened the glove compartment to get my purse and pretended I didn't hear his odd compliment. "What was that?"

"Nothing," he said quickly, throwing the truck into park. "I'll get your door. I don't want anyone getting handsy with you."

"Handsy? What kind of place did you take me to, Klive?"

"I'm joking," he said, turning off the engine. "Just let me be a gentleman and help you from the truck, okay?"

I gave a long-suffering sigh. "If I must."

As he walked around the car, I could hear him berating himself for what he'd said. "Chicken makes you radiant?" I heard him ask. "What, did my brain go on strike tonight? I'm acting as if I've never been around a female before. Well, maybe I haven't been around one as pretty as her, but... Shit, can she hear me?" He blew out a deep breath before opening my door. "Sorry."

I let him help me out of the truck before I asked, "Are you okay? Should I start doubting your mental stability?"

"I'll be fine once I get a beer in me," he said, giving me a wink.

I laughed. "Care to make a wager on that?

*** 

For the rest of my immortal life, I'll never forget the night Klive and I walked into Dancing Bob's Bar and Grill. The second we opened the battered lime-green door, every eye in the room turned our way. Several men even whistled under their breath. I knew that because the entire room fell silent with surprise. The only sound was the door closing behind us and the old George Straight on the jukebox.

Within seconds, a burly, flannel-shirted man stood, smoothed out his hat hair, and sucked in his gut before asking me, "Can I have the next dance, ma'am?"

I looked to Klive with abject fear in my eyes. "Uh, I—I..."

"She's only dancing with me tonight, Bud," Klive told him, putting on his best 'good old boy' drawl.

The man huffed, slapped his hat back on his head, and shuffled back to his barstool without saying a word. My mouth dropped open in surprise. "Okaaay."

"I can't believe that jerk had the nerve to ask you that," Klive said, leading me to the empty side of the room behind the pool table, all the while seething with rage.

"Why is that?" I asked, confused by the whole thing. What had just happened?

He pulled a chair for me and motioned for me to sit. "He knew better. He's a shifter, and you've got my stink on you."

I wrinkled my nose. "Lovely."

"You know what I mean. You smell like my animal, which, by the way, I need to talk to you about. Oswin almost had a heart attack when he found out you didn't know."

"Know what?" I asked warily.

"I'm not a wolf," he said gently. "I'm a were-lion." He sat back in his chair and waited for me to process what he'd laid on me.

"A lion," I repeated. "In a wolf pack?"

"Yeah. I know it's not the most conventional living situation, but the Meridian wolf pack couldn't stand to see me so young and on my own."

"Why were you on your own?"

"My pride decided not only did they not want another male to compete with, they especially didn't want one that had inexplicably inherited an anomaly that makes him phase into a white lion. They didn't want me there, dirtying up their pure, elite gene pool. My aunt sent me to the wolf pack to live with her best friend from college when it was clear bad things were going to happen. She didn't want me to end up dead before my fifth birthday."

Horrified, I whispered, "You were lucky to have an aunt that cared about you that much."

"You don't have to tell me that," he said, more relaxed now that everything was out on the table. "I thank the Lord every day that she was there for me after my parents died."

"That must have been scary for you, having to leave your pride and stay with an entirely different were-animal pack."

He shrugged. "My foster parents and sisters made it feel as normal as possible for me. And in the human world, no one could tell I wasn't related to them."

"You do look amazingly like your sisters."

"I hear that a lot."

"I'll bet. The resemblance is uncanny."

With nothing else to say, an awkward silence fell between us for a few moments before Klive took my hand between his and asked, "So, now that my secret is out, do you still want to have a drink and chicken strips with me?"

I nodded enthusiastically and grinned. "Rum and Coke, please."

Relieved, Klive grinned back and strolled over to the bar to place our order, all the while checking on me in the periphery. I didn't know if it was because he was making sure I was safe or whether he was afraid I'd run screaming from the bar because of the new revelation.

Personally, I didn't think any of those things were going to happen. The crowd didn't even notice us now that we'd been at the bar a few minutes. And I certainly didn't care that he wasn't a wolf, though I had serious doubts I could look at Oswin and Klive together after tonight and not think about the *"human sacrifice, dogs and cats living together... mass hysteria!"* line from Ghostbusters.

"That's a pretty serious face you have on," Klive noted when he came back. "Second thoughts?"

"Nope, thinking about movies," I said, accepting my glass. It wasn't a lie. I had been thinking about a movie … technically.

"Oh, yeah? What kind of movies do you like?"

"All types, but honestly, I mostly watch comedies and romances, sometimes both. What about you?"

He sat across from me and took the straw out of his drink. "Horror, military movies, action movies … typical guy stuff." I cringed, and he laughed. "Not exactly a match made in heaven, huh?"

"That has yet to be determined," I said, smiling as I took a sip of my drink, which was basically all alcohol. Sputtering, I gasped out, "What the hell is this?"

"Long Island Iced Tea. I thought we deserved something a little stronger than rum."

"I'm not sure what I did to deserve that," I said, fighting the urge to grab the guy's beer at the next table to wash the grain alcohol taste out of my mouth. "

Klive grinned. "You'll get used to it in a minute or two."

He was right. After my third sip, I was ready for another one and maybe something else. "Can we get some Tequila shots and lemon?"

"I thought you'd never ask." He waved to the waitress. "Tequila, salt, and lemon, please."

"You got it," she said, straightening her cleavage-bearing shirt to show even more of her breasts.

"I think she likes you," I teased.

"That's too bad," he told me, grinning wickedly. "Because I'm smitten with someone else."

"Oh?"

"Yeah, and she's beautiful tonight."

I blushed and couldn't think of anything to say to that. If anyone else had said it, I probably would have laughed at how thick they were pouring the charm on, but with Klive, I knew he wasn't telling me what I wanted to hear. He was telling me what was in his heart.

A few tequila shots and another Long Island later, our chicken came out from the kitchen, steaming hot and smelling like heaven. "I'm probably going to burn my mouth, but I can't wait," I told Klive, practically drooling. "They smell divine!"

"Bob would've been a chef," he told me, his mouth stretched wide with a grin. "But he couldn't work the hours he needed to on the night of the full moon. This is a much better fit, I think. Plus, he's a bit of a day drinker."

Giggling, I popped a piece of chicken in my mouth and moaned in pleasure. "You weren't kidding. They are so good!"

"I think it's the honey mustard dip that makes them really special. It complements the beer batter perfectly."

"You are so not wrong about that," I said, taking another bite and sighing dramatically.

"Uh, guys?"

We looked up to find our waitress, Cindy, at our table, looking amused. "What's up?" Klive asked, giving her a smile like he was the devil in blue jeans.

"We're all wondering how you're liking those chicken strips."

"They're fantastic!" I gushed. "The best I've ever had."

She leaned in, her breasts crushing together like two overinflated water balloons. "We can tell," she said in a low voice, motioning to the crowd of shifters staring at me while I had a When Harry Met Sally moment with a basket of chicken strips. "The guys want to know if they can buy you some more."

I blushed bright red and mouthed, "No, thank you," to the crowd. They all groaned in disappointment and turned back to their beers. "Sorry," Klive and I said simultaneously.

Cindy was barely holding it together as she tried not to laugh at us. "Can I get y'all anything else?"

"Two more Long Islands, another couple rounds of shots, and the check, if you would," Klive told her.

"Coming right up," she said with a wink. "You two behave yourselves over here."

"Thanks," I called after her, then I looked at Klive and burst into hysterical giggles.

"I guess we should enjoy our food a little less enthusiastically," he said.

"Maybe they shouldn't make such delicious food," I retorted.

Leaning in, Klive brushed his mouth against mine, stealing my breath in a very possessive kiss. "That's a healthy attitude to have," he told me. "But I think a well-placed warning on the menu might be a good idea. Their food seems to make certain individuals nearly orgasmic." He planted another eager kiss to my lips. "You are one hot carnivore."

I burst into laughter again and took a long draw on my straw, nearly choking when he raised his eyebrows and nodded suggestively. "Don't do that!" I screeched.

He slapped me on the back and handed me a napkin from the dispenser. "What are you going to do? Die?"

We tried to stifle more giggles as Cindy unloaded our order on the table. "You two sure are having a good time," she noted.

"They say to live your life to the fullest," I told her.

"That one there looks like he'd fill you up to the fullest, all right," she said, giving Klive an appraising, appreciative glance before strutting away with a little wiggle in her step.

"Did I just get objectified?" Klive asked. He stared at Cindy in mock horror before shaking his head and handing me a shot and a slice of lemon.

"What about the salt?" I asked, my hands full.

"Oh, sorry." He pulled the hand with the lemon slice up to his mouth and licked the delicate web between my thumb and forefinger.

With my mouth parted in desire, I watched as Klive ripped the salt packet open with his teeth and sprinkled a tiny bit onto my wet skin. It was such a simple thing he'd done, but that didn't make it any less effective. It had turned me on.

Klive smiled sheepishly when he caught sight of my dazed expression. "I guess that was a little presumptuous of me."

"No, I…" I trailed off and shifted uncomfortably.

"You what?" he pressed

"I thought your tongue would be rough like a cat's."

"If my tongue was as rough as it is in my animal form, I could do serious damage to your skin."

I nodded to the hand he still held between his. "I'm going to need that back if I'm going to take this shot."

"Sorry," he said, reluctant to let me go.

I licked the salt, took both shots in succession, and bit into the lemon without taking my eyes off the leonine features I'd been too preoccupied to notice before. Klive watched me with a sort of wistful hunger. I had a feeling if he was in cat form right now, his tail would be swishing.

"You mesmerize me," he purred.

"You're drunk," I told him.

"Not quite yet," he said. Lifting my hand to his mouth, he licked the leftover salt from my skin and took the two shots back to back, but instead of using a lemon slice as I had done, he leaned forward and kissed me.

I moaned as he licked open my mouth and dipped inside with his tongue. Encouraged, he threaded his hands in my hair and deepened the kiss. I twisted his shirt in my hands as he lapped at my mouth, needing to touch him, to get closer to his body.

"Ahem," a voice said, breaking the spell. We broke apart, guiltily looking at each other before glancing up at Cindy. "You two are going to have to take this lovefest somewhere else. Harold had to excuse himself to the bathroom to relieve himself if you know what I mean.

I knew exactly what she meant. The scent of my arousal was noticeable even to my vampire senses. "Do you have the number to a cab company?" I asked. "I don't think either one of us is in good enough shape to drive home."

"Where y'all headed?"

"About an hour south," Klive said.

"I suggest you stay at the motel behind the bar. It's clean, and it will cost you a lot less than a cab. Plus, you won't have to make a return trip to get your truck tomorrow."

Klive gave me a questioning look. "What do you think?"

"I think you're going to have to carry me to the motel."

***

The cold hit us like a wall of stinging pain as we stepped out of the bar. With all the alcohol we'd drank and the heated glances we'd been throwing at each other tonight, I'd forgotten how cold the temperature was going to be. "Brrrr," I complained, my teeth chattering.

He stripped out of his jacket and threw it over my shoulders. "Come on, I can see the sign from here," he said, leading me toward a motel that looked like it had its heyday in the nineteen-seventies and hadn't been updated since ... or painted ... or cleaned.

"Are you sure there aren't any hatchet-wielding serial killers in there?"

He snickered. "Korrina, you're a vampire-nymph, and I'm a lion, I think we can take 'em."

"I'm not at my best," I said, wobbling in my heels. "And why did you say vampire like that?"

"Like what?"

"Like you're Count Dracula."

"But I am," he exclaimed in a terrible accent. "And I want to suck your blood!" He pulled me closer and gave me a playful bite on my neck.

"Something tells me you want more than that," I said, looking pointedly at the sizable bulge in his jeans.

He nodded to the motel and laughed. "I cannot go in there like this."

"Think about something to get rid of it," I told him, giggling at his predicament.

"Like what?"

I squinted in the distance at the headlights coming closer and every bit of lust drained out of my body. "Think about the fact that Oswin is about fifteen seconds away."

"Yeah, that ought to do it," he said. "Can you imagine if he really were?"

"He is," I told him, pointing at the werewolf's pickup truck pulling up in front of us.

# SAVING HER FROM HERSELF
## OSWIN

With the truck barely stopped, I jumped out, stormed over to Korrina, and threw her over my shoulder. She was so drunk; she didn't even try resist. She just let me put her into the truck through the driver's side and watched openmouthed as I slid in next to her, started the engine, and drove away from a thoroughly pissed Klive.

"What the hell, Oswin?" she asked, her eyes wide.

Incredulous, I spoke through clenched teeth. "I should ask you the same, Korrina. What the hell are you doing with Klive?"

I immediately regretted the note of homicidal rage that tinged my voice. It would set her off, but damn it, I had a right to know. She was *my* mate, *mine*. Seeing her tonight, wrapped in Klive's arms, in his jacket, I just couldn't take it. I was ready to murder him, no matter the pack laws.

When she stayed quiet, I asked, "Cat got your tongue?"

"He would!" she exploded. "I can't believe you, dragging me away like a fucking caveman!"

"You can't believe me?" I roared.

"You don't want me!" she yelled back. "You never did. It's all just mind games and bullshit with you, Oswin!"

"I don't want you," I repeated bitterly. "I don't want you? Are you fucking kidding me?" Slamming on the brakes, I guided the truck to a stop in a deserted Sunoco station parking lot and turned off the ignition. "You know what, Korrina? Fuck you."

"Fuck me?" she asked, more livid than I'd ever seen her before.

I met her electric green eyes and spoke slowly, "Yeah, darlin'. Fuck. You."

She didn't say anything, only unbuckled her seatbelt and leaped from the passenger side toward me. Her mouth crashed into mine as she frantically tried to unzip my jeans. I tugged her dress up as she worked to free my cock, smiling against her lips when I found she was bare and ready for me.

"Please," she moaned, writhing against me as she rubbed her warm wetness along my hard length. "Please, Oswin."

Arms tight around her waist, I positioned her over my cock and impaled her on it, swallowing her cries of pain and pleasure with a deep, searching kiss. I felt lost in a sea of lust, righteous anger, and love for my mate as I moved in her, lifting her knees off the seat with the ferocity of my thrusts. She held on tight to me, nails digging into my shoulders, as she matched the movements that were quickly bringing us to orgasm.

Growling, I slid a hand into her dark curls and yanked her head back, asserting control. "Come for me, Korrina."

Eyes dark and hungry, she convulsed around me, screaming out my name as she reached her climax, then she collapsed bonelessly onto my chest. "Oswin?"

I wrapped her in my arms and buried my face in her hair, breathing in the scent I'd missed so much. "Yeah, darlin'?"

"Passing out," she slurred, her slight weight becoming limp.

"Korrina?" I shook her shoulder a little. She whimpered and snuggled into my neck. I leaned my head back onto the headrest and laughed. Four years I'd waited to be intimate with my mate, and she'd fallen asleep in the middle of it.

Gently lifting her off my erection, I placed her back into her seat, straightened her dress before I buckled her seatbelt, and threw my coat over her. She burrowed into the collar and sighed contentedly before falling back asleep.

Settling back in my own seat, I glanced down at my hard dick. "It's been almost four years," I told it. "What's a few more hours?"

I woke with a start when I felt Korrina's soft hand on my chest. "What's wrong?" I asked her, my voice gravelly with sleep. I was surprised she was awake. She'd been passed out cold since I tucked her into my bed a few hours earlier.

Several seconds passed with no response, prompting me to crack an eye open to see if she'd fallen back asleep. Her eyes were closed, but her mouth was parted, and her breathing was accelerated. She wanted me.

No sooner than the thought crossed my mind, her hand dipped lower, resting below my navel. My cock jumped in anticipation, brushing against her hand and making her breath catch. She opened her green eyes, looking hungry for me.

I grinned down at her. "Is there something I can help you with, Korrina?"

Slowly, she pulled her dress over her head and nodded. "Yes, please."

I dove for her mouth, wedging my hips between her legs and brushing soft, tentative kisses across her lips. She moaned and arched against me, causing my erection to press into her center in a very pleasurable way. Gasping, she deepened the kiss, groaning in ecstasy as I slowly slid inside. Over and over, I plunged into her with sure, deliberate strokes. With pride, I watched her as she met my thrusts, eyes tightly shut as she cried out in pleasure. Nothing made me happier than being able to give her this.

"Come inside me," she said in a breathy voice, her movements becoming erratic as she reached her peak. "Now, Oswin!"

Bracketing her legs around my waist, I lifted her thighs and pounded into her with abandon, thrusting harder and harder until I roared out my completion, spilling deep inside of her. Blissfully spent, I collapsed onto my elbows, smiling down at my mate before kissing her long and deep.

She threaded her hands in my hair as I lifted my head. "I love you."

I froze and stared into her eyes, my heart swelling with love for my beautiful female. "Korrina, there will never be anyone but you. I'll never love anyone else. I don't care how many consorts you take.

Chewing her lip, she said, "Oswin, the vision is right; I do have feelings for Klive, but it's … not the same as it is between us." She met my gaze. "Thank you for coming for me. I'm not sure I'm ready to do what we were about to do."

I slipped out of her, rolled us until she was cuddled to my chest, and gave a low chuckle. "I'll always come for you, Korrina."

# AN UNEXPECTED HOUSEGUEST
## KORRINA

I was on my way home from Oswin's with the mother of all hangovers and a heavyweight of confusion and guilt on my shoulders when the Addams Family theme song erupted from my phone. Obsidian was finally calling me! Squealing, I swiped the screen and answered with a breathless, "Hello?"

*"Did I catch you at a bad time?"* Obsidian asked. His voice sounded tinny and far away. And it didn't sound happy.

"You could have caught me a little sooner," I scolded. "I think I might be a little upset with you. You promised to call when your plane landed, you know. That was three days ago."

*"I apologize, my love. I forgot to bring the outlet adapter for my phone charger. You wouldn't believe how remote these orchards are. I'm glad I packed blood. There's not a store or shop for miles. I finally canceled the meeting with the Bloomington's to take a taxi to the nearest town with more than fifty people. It cost me nearly eighty-seven euros for this thing."*

I laughed. For a vampire, Obsidian could be a little forgetful. It was kind of adorable, really. "You're forgiven."

*"And you're a saint,"* he said, relief coloring his voice. *"But I was sure Oswin would tell you that we spoke on your first night back?"*

"You called him, but not me?"

*"He called me. In quite the panic, I might add. It seems you regained the upper hand."*

"And then some," I told him. "When you get home, we need to talk."

*"Are you okay?"*

"Yeah, but … uh, how do you feel about kids?"

*"Are you…"* he trailed off as if he was afraid to utter the word.

I blew out a breath. *"No, but I will be."*

*"Errr … is that some kind of nymph thing?"* he asked. *"I don't understand."*

"I don't either. This is all bizarre, new territory to me. Just know that everything is going smoothly between Oswin and me and that I'm adjusting as best as I can to not having my husband and best friends around to keep me normal."

*"You can always talk to Oswin,"* he suggested.

I sighed. "I said things were going smooth, not perfect."

*"It'll take time, love, but you'll get there."*

"We'll see."

*"So, how is it going at the house?"* he asked.

"Fine," I hedged, not wanting to delve into the fact that I hadn't spent more than a couple hours there since I arrived. "I still don't understand why we're not living in our own house."

He laughed. *"Korrina, you do realize they're both our houses, right?"*

"You know what I mean. I feel like your parents are going to come down here and kick me out their four-poster in my jammies."

He chuckled. *"That's not likely to happen. They haven't been back to Goshen to visit in nearly seventy years."*

"Yeah, but you never know. Are you sure we shouldn't stay at yours, just in case?"

*"I take it you haven't been by the other house since you've arrived."*

"No. Why?"

*"Drop by there. You'll see."*

I huffed. "That's a little unhelpful, oh man of mystery."

He laughed again. *"I will see you very soon, my love."*

"Soon, eh?"

*"Yes."*

"When you get here, will you be continuing with this cryptic form of communication?" I asked.

*"Maybe,"* he conceded.

"You're an awful vampire. You know that?"

*"Yes, I do. Now go get some rest before the run tonight."*

"How did you know the pack was running tonight?"

*"Because I'm hours ahead of Alabama, love. The moon is as full as a plate tonight."*

I laughed at myself. "Oh, yeah. Well, I feel like an idiot."

He joined me in my laughter then said, *"You are far from an idiot, Korrina, which is why I know you will keep yourself out of trouble tonight. Stay high in the trees if you follow along. You're safest up there."*

"Yes, sir."

*"I love you, Korrina."*

"I love you, too, Obsidian."

As soon as the line went dead, I hit end and had an all-out panic attack. What had I been thinking, naming Klive my consort? It changed my entire life's course. What if Obsidian didn't want kids with two other guys? What if he divorced me because of all this? I couldn't lose him; he was my sire. I didn't think I'd make it a day without knowing, beyond the shadow of a doubt, that we would be together forever. Obsidian was my rock, my touchstone.

*"Oh, Korrina,"* soothed a huge American Beech, its yellow-leafed branches reaching to console me. *"Calm yourself. Things will work to your favor. The vampire loves you."*

102

Eager to accept the consolation, I wrapped my arms around the tree and squeezed.

Yes, I hugged a tree.

I may have had to pick leaves out of my hair afterward, but it was worth it. I walked away feeling focused and happy, which, let's face it, was a miracle at this point.

Once I was clear-headed, I realized the answer to my problems was to call Sapphire. She'd know exactly what I needed to do. Yanking my phone out of my purse, I dialed her number and prayed that she wasn't at some fancy vampire party with Kieran or having her own party with her husband—the naked kind of party. Either was possible.

*"Hello?"*

I breathed a sigh of relief. "Hey, Saph. It's me."

*"Who's me?"* she asked.

"Saph, come on. Look at the caller ID, for Pete's sake."

*"The caller ID said this was my one of my best friends, but you can't be her. My best friend wouldn't forget to call me for days, especially when she knew how worried I was about her moving next door to a wolf pack."*

"Your best friend also wouldn't name Oswin's second her consort and then find out that she's going to have younglings," I retorted. "It's been a hell of a couple days, Sapphire."

*"You're pregnant?"* she screeched.

"No, but I will be. Oswin's pack has a seer. She told me my fate."

*"And you believed her?"* she demanded. *"Are you insane? High? Stupid?"*

"I must be," I grumbled. "I call someone who thinks I'm stupid my best friend."

*"Give me a second to let this sink in! I was expecting a few days of dirty sex with Oswin, not a wolf pup."*

"Klive isn't a wolf, and I haven't had sex with him, yet."

There was silence on her end for a second. *"What?"*

"He's a were-lion. And the seer is right. I can feel it."

She took a deep breath. *"Oh, okay."*

It was no surprise that Sapphire didn't question how I knew the seer was right. She'd long ago chalked all the weird happenings in my life up to "creepy supernatural stuff" and took it with a grain of salt. I tried to remind her that she was now smack dab in the middle of all that creepy supernatural stuff, but she was still pretending she was human.

"Shit, Saph. I almost forgot to tell you the best part. I fucked Oswin last night, twice."

She laughed. *"So, it has been a busy couple of days."*

"You have no idea."

*"All right. Here's what I think you should do,"* she said, moving into problem-solving mode.

I sighed in relief, embarrassingly glad that I had someone to help me live my life. "Tell me, Yoda."

*"This may be beyond Yoda's help,"* she said thoughtfully.

"Spill it, lady."

*"All right. Where are you right now? I hear crickets."*

"I'm in the woods outside my house."

*"Why? Never mind. Of course, you are. Okay, first things first. You need to go to the store. Buy hot chocolate, the fixings for homemade mac and cheese, wine, blood, and a big bottle of a good Irish whiskey."*

"Is that Kieran's influence?" I asked, thinking of the enigmatic Irish vampire.

*"Are you questioning my methods?"*

"I'll buy the whiskey," I said meekly. "What else?"

*"Movies,"* she said. *"None of that sappy, romantic stuff, either. You need Pitch Perfect, Mean Girls, and The House Bunny. Maybe, Netflix a season or two of Gilmore Girls."*

"Okay, got it."

*"Oh, and fuzzy flannel pajamas. Do you have those?"*

"No, but I could get some at Walmart."

*"Do it. You get bonus points if you can find Christmas pajamas."*

I laughed. "Now it's a mission!"

*"Good. Call me when you get back, okay?"*

"Okay. Thanks, Saph."

*"What are friends for?"*

"Damned if I know." I sighed. "I wish you were here."

*"Me, too,"* she said. *"Love you, Korrina."*

"Love you, too. I'll call you soon."

*"I'll be here. Bye."*

"Bye." I hung up the phone and smiled. I was right. She knew exactly what to do.

***

Two hours later, I stepped out onto the porch with a cup of hot chocolate, clean and sweet smelling. I was wearing my flannel Santa Claus pajamas as instructed and had Mean Girls set to play on my streaming device. I was all ready to take my mind off my problems.

Sitting in the porch chair I'd pulled out of the storage pod, I rocked as I stared down the driveway, enjoying the crisp bite of the evening. After only a few seconds of contentment, I realized I was rocking my chair to the faint rhythm of music. Stilling the motion, I listened intently. The music seemed to be coming from our other house. But who could be playing it? Had Obsidian rented our house to someone without telling me? Was that the reason he said I should check it out?

I let my curiosity get the better of me, just like I had so many years ago with Obsidian. Setting my cup on the porch railing, I padded down the steps in my pink fuzzy slippers and made my way closer to the thick brush and trees between our two houses. Assured that it was, in fact, coming from our house, I changed direction and wandered through the forest toward the sound of Jason Aldean's warbling voice, half-ignoring the comments and concerns of the many trees as I made my way through.

I stopped short when I arrived at the house and saw a werewolf with inky black hair and an extremely nice ass. His tall form was stretched into a strong, practiced arch as he balanced on the safety rail of his scaffold to reach the eaves he was painting. Too terrified to move or speak, I waited with bated breath as he finished the corner and made his way to the ground. Werewolf or not, I didn't want to startle him. It was a long way down.

"You can come closer now," the werewolf male said, smirking in my direction. His voice was deep and utterly Louisianan. "But I do appreciate you making sure I didn't fall to my death and all."

A slow smile spread across my face. I'd been a sucker for a Louisiana accent ever since the first time I saw Gambit on an old X-men episode. "You're welcome. Thanks for not ripping my throat out before I could introduce myself."

He stuck out a hand and met me halfway across the yard. "Luke Rivette," he said. His straight, sharp white teeth gleamed in the moonlight.

"Korrina Raines."

"Oh, I know who you are. You've been the talk of the pack for the past couple of days. Well, that, and your scent is pure nymph."

"Talk of the pack?" I asked casually. He gave me a stark look. I sighed. "Yeah, I know. I'm the foretold grandmother of the future Alpha or whatever."

He raised a dark eyebrow.

Man, this guy was good with the facial expressions. I was incapable of resisting those baby blues. They made me want to spill my guts and tell him everything.

"Look, Luke, I'd be lying if I said I was happy with the way things are turning out. A few months ago, I was perfectly happy with Obsidian and Obsidian only. I mean, Oswin isn't really turning out to be the burden I thought he might be, but that still doesn't change the fact that I would be happier if my husband were my only mate." I paused and took a deep breath. "Sorry, I don't mean to bother you with my troubles."

He ignored the comment and asked, "And the lion?"

"The lion is … unexpected," I told him. "But not entirely unwelcome." I looked up and didn't have to search for compassion in his countenance. "Luke, I think I might love him."

Surprise flittered across his face before he was able to regain the blank but concerned expression he'd been wearing. "You do?"

Smiling wearily, I said, "I can't help myself. I love them all."

"A hazard of your race?" he asked, sounding uncannily like Obsidian had when he'd asked me that question years ago.

"No, I think, in this case, the blame lies squarely on the shoulders of fate. At least, that what Thusnelda says."

"Fate can be a real bitch," Luke told me. The near angry look on his face told me that that particular bitch had visited his house on more than one occasion.

"Tell me about it," I agreed.

Shaking off the fog of his thoughts, he asked, "So, what can I do for you, Korrina? Or should I call you Alpha, or landlady, or maybe, mother of our advanced civilization?"

I squinted at him.

"Okay, not that last one," he conceded.

"Thank you."

"So, did your car break down?"

Confused, I stared at him. "What?"

He jerked his head toward a tow truck proclaiming "Luke's Towing" in a fancy font. "I drive a wrecker. Folks usually come here for a tow."

"Oh," I said stupidly, laughing and rolling my eyes. "No. I heard the music. Obsidian didn't tell me he'd rented the house."

Nodding, he seemed to relax a bit. "I moved in a few weeks after y'all moved to Virginia."

"A few weeks? But ... how?"

"How did I know my pack would move here?"

"Yeah."

"I didn't. I joined the pack afterward."

"But you don't want to live on the pack-lands or participate in the community?"

He shook his head, starting to walk back to the ladder. "I'm more of a lone wolf, Mrs. Raines."

"By choice?" I asked. He spoke with a tough guy attitude, but I didn't buy it. I knew his secret; the trees told me as soon as I started for his house.

He didn't answer the question, he only said, "Well, I got to get back to this."

Translation: "You can go, Korrina. You're dismissed."

"All right, lone wolf," I called after him. "But just so you know, I already know the answer. I was giving you the opportunity to share with me as I did with you. That's what friends do."

He stopped mid-step and turned around. "Oh, we're friends now, are we?"

"We will be. Soon as you lighten up."

He wore a disbelieving expression. "Is that another one of Thusnelda's predictions?"

Closing the distance between us, I slipped my arms around his waist to hug him. "Nope. It's mine."

"What are you doing?" he asked, a note of amusement in his gruff voice.

"Shhhh," I told him and hugged him tighter, laying my cheek on his flannel-covered chest.

After a few frozen seconds, he wrapped his arms around me, nuzzled his face into my hair, and we just stood there, two strangers wrapped around each other for comfort. Eventually, we both shed tears. Me, because of the turn of events. Him, because of the great loss of his wife and mate. We were both hurt, both scared, and we both needed someone who was removed from the drama, someone who wasn't entangled in her death or my future.

Raw, but soothed, we straightened and stared at each other. He wiped at his eyes and sniffed. I didn't even bother trying to clean myself up. It would take a damp washcloth to remove the dried blood trailing down my cheeks.

He pulled a folded bandanna out of his back pocket and poured half a bottle of water over it. Handing it to me, he asked, "How did you know?"

"The trees told me."

His eyes darted to the tree-line. "They really talk to you?"

"They can speak to anyone. But it tends to freak out the humans."

"And werewolves," he added. "Is it out loud or do they speak in your head?"

"Both for me. Out loud for you. As a nymph, I have a connection that allows their magic to cycle through me. The silent conversations are one of the perks."

He pursed his lips. "So, what exactly did the trees tell you about me?"

I grimaced. "Are you sure you want to know? You'll never feel like you have privacy again."

He took a second to think it over. "Yes. I want to know."

*"'Luke is a widower,'* I said in my best rendition of the tree's ethereal voices. *'He is alone and laments the loss of his mate. We ask that you extend your hand in friendship in our stead.'"*

He sat in the patio chair hard. "They think I need a friend?"

"Apparently."

He laughed bitterly. "My mate always told me I needed to make more friends."

I knelt next to him and laid my hand on his knee. His calloused palm covered mine, and he gave me a small smile.

"She died ten days before I moved in here," he told me quietly. "She was quite a bit older than me, but I was so damn sure we'd have more time together."

"I'm so sorry," I said, my heart breaking for him. "No one should have to go through the pain of losing their mate."

He pinned me with an honest stare. "If you really believe that, you'll have those kids. Spreading the immortality gene is the only way to ensure the wolves survival."

"You've been thinking about this a lot, haven't you?"

He smiled lasciviously. "Not all of us have been tasked with making the pups. Some of us have to be content with focusing on the outcome."

I quirked my lips. "I think I liked you better when you were surly."

A genuine smile, the first one I'd seen from him, spread across his face. He stood and offered me a hand up. "See you later, friend. This painting ain't going to finish itself."

"Need some help?"

"Naw. You go on and get cleaned up before the run. You look like a walking horror movie."

I swiped the dampened bandanna across my cheek and sighed at the spread of blood across the light blue fabric. Stupid vampire tears.

# STOP RUNNING AWAY FROM YOUR FEELINGS
## OSWIN

The night was blessedly cool as I made my way to the meadow I'd chosen for our meeting spot. I couldn't help but be thankful for it. Anything that would make tonight's run smoother was a good thing. I wanted Korrina's first run with the pack to be perfect.

On top of a small hill, I came to a stop, looking down at the smiling, happy wolves milling around the clearing. It was obvious they were more than ready to stretch their legs. And that was doubly true for the pups. They were doing what came naturally to them; most had already phased and were running around, barking and yipping their heads off with glee because they were up way, way past their bedtime. Their parents, however, were giving each other amused, commiserating grimaces when they weren't rolling their eyes at Peter, who was telling anyone who would listen how he was going to 'get that bear' this time.

Pleased at the favorable turnout, I shook my head at their antics and chuckled to myself before my eyes shot to the trees to my left. Korrina had arrived. I couldn't see her or smell her scent, but I could sense her through our bond. With a burst of speed, I jogged down the hill and called for the pack's attention. Despite the sudden, marked need to see my mate, I decided to watch Klive and Korrina cross the field like a lovesick fool was a little on the stalkerish side and didn't set a good precedent.

"Huddle up, guys," I called, waiting a few seconds for them to quieten down. "All right. First, I want to say thanks to y'all for coming out. I know some of you would rather be spending time with your friends instead of being here doing the traditional thing with the pack, so, thanks."

Candace and Brent's four-year-old son, Jonah, raised his hand with excited enthusiasm. "I know the rules, Mr. Oswin. Can I say them this time?"

I grinned at the tow-headed little tyke and called him over to stand with me. "Let's have it then, Jonah."

He turned to the crowd and lisped, "We can't go past the boundary fences, and Mr. Peter can't go after the bear."

I ruffled his hair and made a shooing motion at the pack. "You heard him. Go on. Have fun. But be back here in time for the headcount at dawn. Don't make me have to track you down, Peter. You'll be lugging sacks of concrete for a week."

The group laughed at Peter's grumbles and starting undressing, carefully folding their clothes and putting them in their backpacks, until they noticed their new Alpha was doing the same. They all stared at her in wonder, apparently ignorant of a nymph's preference to be nude while enjoying time in the forest. With her vampiric vision and hearing, Korrina had to know she was being watched and talked about, but she didn't acknowledge it or show any sign of nervousness as she shed her skirt and straightened with an expectant look at Klive, who was still fully dressed and staring at her naked body in awe.

"Are you going to undress?" she asked him. When he didn't react, she giggled and snapped her fingers in front of his face.

He snapped his teeth at her fingers and laughed. "Sorry. It's just ... wow."

"Well, brace yourself," she told him. "I'm not done yet."

"Oh, yeah? I..." Klive's sarcastic retort turned into a gasp that was echoed by nearly everyone in the pack.

"Don't freak out," she pleaded, her voice ethereal and nearly otherworldly as her features became angular, slanting in an almost alien angle. Klive nodded, staring openmouthed as her long dark hair came to life with delicate vines that spiraled down to her feet before bursting into full bloom. Petals of snow white swirled around them before fading into nothingness.

"Whoa," he said, reaching out to gingerly touch her face and hair. "How is it possible that you're more beautiful?"

Korrina stood on the tips of her toes to kiss his cheek. "You know, I think I'll keep you." She pointed to the tree limb high above her. "I'm going up. You coming?"

"Right behind you," he told her, unzipping his pants. "Just give me a second to phase." He grinned. "Don't freak out, okay?"

Grinning back at him, she stood tall, reaching above her head in a practiced fifth position to allow vines that were twisting down from the tree to lift her to a high, sturdy branch. "Don't worry," she called. "I won't."

Our eyes met as the vines retreated, and I nodded to her, holding my breath and trying like hell to school my expression as my jealousy spiked. I wanted to be the one in the trees with her tonight … so much, it hurt my chest.

Returning the motion, she mouthed, "Soon," and smiled, her hair bursting into bloom again. The petals scattered in the breeze, peppering the hillside I stood on. As I watched the soft, magical caresses fade on the bare skin of my chest, I smiled to myself, sure, for the first time in four years, that she was starting to forgive me.

A pained grunt and the sharp crack of bone drew our attention back to Klive. On his hands and knees, his change roiled over him like molten golden metal. Roaring, he shook himself and shot up the tree after her. Like dominos, the pack followed his lead, shifting into their wolves and taking off into the distance with howls and excited barks. Dropping to my own knees, I clenched my teeth and let my wolf take over. As much as I wanted to follow them as they hopped limb to limb, someone had to stay behind to watch the rest of the pack-lands while the others ran the back fifty thousand acres. I couldn't risk the safety of the pack because I was jealous, not when we were at our most vulnerable.

Resigned, I trotted the opposite direction and followed a few of the pups to the creek they liked to splash around in. Once I was reassured they were being watched, I turned my attention to the boundary fences. The smell of satyr became overwhelming the closer I came to the east end of the fence. Huffing out a breath, I sat on my haunches and watched the trees sway in the wind as I tried to place the direction Agapios come from.

I thought maybe his smell originated from the north. Kieran Kinane had purchased the land with my blessing shortly after I moved the pack, and he had already started clearing the land. It was a safe bet the satyr was taking the easy route. Otherwise, Korrina would have been made aware of his presence by the trees in his path.

With it clear that I had a threat on my hands, I made a mental note to call Kieran and get him to install cameras during his build and to have Korrina ask the boundary trees what they'd seen before taking off to check the rest of the fence. Any hunting my wolf wanted to do would have to wait. My pack had to come first.

# LUPINE AND FELINE BEHAVIOR

## KORRINA

Watching Klive jump from tree to tree in his cat form was somewhat of a surreal experience. His lithe movements were a thing of beauty, so at odds with the pensive personality I'd become accustomed to. Like the flip of a switch, the shy male I'd come to know was gone. In his place, a pure-white surefooted animal whose coat shone like satin in the moonlight, wild and untamed.

After ten or fifteen minutes of taking in the general beauty of his feline form, I swung to the limb he'd settled on and asked, "Can you understand me like this?"

A nod of his huge head came before he nuzzled my arm and purred.

I reached around him and cuddled him close, enjoying the vibrations. "You're so beautiful, Klive. Far more impressive than these ordinary wolves."

He yawned and gave me a look that said, "Of course, I am. I'm a lion."

I watched the wolves spread out below us and smiled at the pups stalking and chasing each other with zeal. "The kids sure are having a good time," I mused.

Klive sat on his haunches and let out a low growl that grew into a quick, warning roar.

Alarmed, I took a step back. "What's going on Klive?"

He didn't answer, only bristled as he stared down at the pups and let out another roar, this time positioning himself to pounce when he was done.

"Klive what are you doing?" I yelled, now officially panicked at what I was seeing. Was I actually going to have to stop him from attacking children?

No doubt distracted by the shrillness of my voice, he turned his head to me and winked.

I squinted at him. "Don't you dare."

But he didn't hear me. He had already jumped down into the gaggle of pups and was stalking them as they ran around like chickens with their heads cut off. Clearly, this was something he did all the time.

"Klive, you behave yourself," I called after him, smiling warmly at the sight of him playing so carefully with the littlest ones.

"He was born to be a dad," a voice said from behind me.

Squeaking, I nearly fell from the branch, but Oswin grabbed my arm and yanked me back to safety. "Oswin! You scared the life out of me!" I yelled, smacking his shoulder.

He grinned. "That's impossible."

I huffed as I sat down, glad we were on a beech tree. A pine would've been a little uncomfortable in my state of undress. "You know what I mean."

"That, I do, darlin'." He glanced down to Klive, who was carrying a wayward pup in his mouth. "He always spends time with the pups during the full moon."

I frowned. "Well, it's not as if he's going to find a mate out there with one of the lady wolves."

"True enough," Oswin said, looking nervous as he perched next to me on the branch.

I sighed. "It's kind of sad, isn't it?"

"I don't think he's too worried about it right now."

"What's that supposed to mean?"

"You know what I mean," he said, throwing my words back at me.

I met his gaze. "Jealous?"

He stared at me, stone-faced. "Exceedingly."

I shrugged. "I hope you aren't expecting any sympathy from me. Because you're not going to get it."

"Didn't think I would," he shot back.

"Then I'm glad to see you're finally paying attention."

He sighed. "Is it always going to be like this between us?"

"Like what?"

"All the bickering and hostility. I know you love me, Korrina. You said so yourself, twice."

I raised my brows. "So, you have been listening."

"Yes, but have you been listening? There is nothing I do that isn't for you. I built these pack-lands for you. I'm suffering through this prophecy and your marriage to Obsidian for you. I'm in love with you."

I blew out a deep breath. "I know, Oswin. Just give me time. I just need more a little more time."

His expression softened. "If time is what you need, darlin', time is what you'll get."

"Thank you," I said, slipping my arms around him. "I know how hard this must be for you."

He chuckled. "It ain't easy, but for you, Korrina, I'd do anything."

# STRANGER DANGER
## OSWIN

At the first signs of dawn, I padded back to the meeting spot to count heads and found Thusnelda waiting there for me. It wasn't strange to see her there. Though she couldn't run with the pack anymore, she liked to spend as much time with them as possible. She said it made her feel like less of a magical freak.

Lowering my muzzle, I greeted her with the wolfy version of a bow, then willed myself back into my human form. "Mornin', Thusnelda."

"Good morning," she said, her face drawn and worried. I could tell she had something she was anxious to say.

"What's wrong?" I asked without preamble.

"It's the satyr Klive mentioned. He's up to something. I just know it. I can't see what it is, but the malice is there. It's definitely there."

I nodded. I'd smelled his scent around the boundaries. "Do you know when he'll strike?"

She laid a hand on my arm and gave me a meaningful look. "I'm afraid he already has. Now go put on some pants and deal with it."

\*\*\*

A few hours later, I sat in a red pleather booth in the bar and grill with the closest proximity to the local mall. To the layman's eye, I probably appeared to be on my downward spiral, drinking a beer at three in the afternoon, but I had a plan ... sort of. I'd heard through the grapevine that Korrina would be shopping with Klive's sisters today. They always had pre-shopping excursion margaritas. I figured if I could casually meet up with Korrina at the bar, she wouldn't feel so ambushed. It seemed like that was the only way we'd been seeing each other lately.

Two beers later, I lifted my gaze from my beer bottle when I felt a prickling of excitement shoot through me like lightning. Korrina was close by. Surveying the room, I saw four of Klive's sisters stepping into the smoky sports bar, the sun turning their blonde hair into halos around their innocent, angelic faces. And trailing behind the tall females was none other than the very vampire-nymph I came here to see.

"Holy shit!" a young human exclaimed as the door to the bar swung open. The man elbowed his two buddies. "Tonight's our lucky night, guys."

I shook my head at the man's misguided ego and watched the party closely, waiting for trouble to come to the ladies. I didn't have to wait long.

As a testament to the lack of women in the greater Goshen area, it didn't take more than four minutes for three human men to work up the nerve to talk to the group of giggling females. The humans couldn't hear their conversation as I could, but if they could, they might not be so cocky in their approach. The females weren't appreciating the view; they were pricing them out like slabs of beef. I'd never heard them speak like this. It was equal parts fascinating and horrifying.

The tallest of the three dark-haired men sidled up to their table. "Good evening, ladies. I'm Cody, and this is Logan and Hunter. Can we buy y'all a drink?"

"I don't know, Cody," Kalista said cheekily. "Can you buy us a drink?"

Hunter laughed loudly. "You had that coming, hoss," He turned his smarmy smile on Kalista's older sister, Keona. "May we buy you ladies a drink?"

Keona preened under his attention. "Yes, you may. It's margaritas all around."

I watched as Logan jerked his head for his friends to follow him to the bar without saying a word and I narrowed my eyes. There was something not quite right about him. There was something sharp and menacing in his smile, something evil. And he wasn't the only one. I had a strong suspicion these 'good ol' boys' weren't at all as they seemed. And if I was right, the females of the pack would never again step foot in this bar without a male escort. I would make sure of it.

Determined to get to the bottom of it, I stood and walked to the bar under the pretense of getting a fresh beer. "Another beer, please," I called to the bartender. "When you get a sec."

Within seconds, I had their scheme worked out. As far as date rape scams went, this one was well thought out, and apparently, had been done before with some success. Hunter and Cody distracted the girls and bartender with a fight over who would pay for the drinks, while Logan quickly drugged them with a medicine dropper and took the tray to the table. It was a slick trick; I had to hand it to them. You know, before I handed them their asses for messing with my pack.

If not for the smoky room, their werewolf senses might have been able to pick up on the bitter smell of the additive, and the females would have shown them a lesson they'd never forget. Sadly, they only chatted sweetly and made cow eyes at Logan as he distributed the drinks among them. When he got to Korrina, her eyes went large and then suspicious. She, however, remained aloof, which didn't sit well with Logan.

"What's the matter, baby? Cat got your tongue?"

"Something exactly like that," Keely said, laughing at their inside joke.

Smiling at the presumptuous human and then over at me, Korrina bared her fangs. "It's actually a wolf that's got my tongue."

Logan bounded up from where he'd cozied up next to her. "Did you say a wolf? Like, a werewolf?"

"Yes," she answered coolly.

The initial shock wore off, he leaned over the back of the chair and smiled. "So, pretty thing, you're a werewolf?"

I tapped him on the shoulder. "No, she isn't. But I am. Oswin Morris," I told him, introducing myself with my own dramatic show of fangs. "And this is my mate, Korrina."

Wide-eyed, the human spun around and sputtered, "S-sorry, man. I didn't know," before going back to his table, slamming his beer, and then leaving without another look at Cody or Hunter. Seeing him hightail it out of the bar, they were quick to follow him.

Kiara crossed her arms and glared at me as the door swung shut behind the human men. "You're an ass, Oswin. Just because you're not getting any doesn't mean you have to ruin it for the rest of us."

I raised my brows. "Kiara, I thought that you and your sisters might be a little more appreciative that I ran off the guys that spiked your drinks in hopes of raping you, or wearing your skin, or whatever they planned to do with your unconscious bodies," I growled through clenched teeth, furious at her impudence, then lowered my voice to barely above a whisper. "And I might remind you that though I have been fodder around the fire for the past few days, I am still your Alpha. I demand respect from my pack."

All of the Williams sisters looked adequately chastised for their indignant behavior, especially Kiara, but not Korrina. No, my mate was smiling at me with pride. We locked eyes for a split second, and I felt dazed like I'd been struck by lightning and my brain had gotten scrambled. I took an unsure step toward her then hesitated. I wanted to say something to her, but I had no idea what that was.

Shaking off the odd feeling, I nodded politely to my mate, strode to the bartender to give him a few words of caution about the three that had left, and went back to my corner booth. It wasn't easy walking away. Leaving the females alone at their table after something like that was nearly impossible. It was written into my DNA to protect my pack with my life.

"Oswin?"

I looked up from the label I was peeling off my beer. Korrina was standing ten feet away, looking reluctant to come any closer. "What can I do for you, darlin'?"

"I wanted to say thank you. Kiara's too proud to say it, but I know she's glad you were there to take care of us."

"Anyone would have done it," I told her, secretly thrilled that we were continuing the tenuous rapport we'd enjoyed since the night we'd been intimate.

She shook her head and stepped a few feet closer. "You and I both know that's not true."

I patted the padded seat next to me. We were almost within touching distance now. "Well, the pack is my responsibility. I have to protect them any way I can."

She leaned over the table, giving me a full view of her creamy white cleavage. "Oswin?"

"Yeah?"

"Will you meet me at your house in three hours?" she asked, barely breathing.

I nodded. "I'll be there."

Korrina left me with a smile and went back to the girls after I gave her my answer. Immediately, they ducked their heads together to whisper about what had happened. That was definitely my cue to leave. They couldn't properly dissect the situation with me there watching them like a hawk. Slamming my beer, I set it on the bar and slipped out the door just as they were getting their non-tainted drinks on the house.

***

True to her word, Korrina showed up on my doorstep three hours later. Sending up a prayer, I let her in and waited for her to speak her mind.

"Oswin..." she started, her voice trailing off as if she was unable to finish. Clearing her throat, she looked up with deep green eyes that tilted in the corners and said, "I want you."

"I'm right here, darlin'."

Without another word, she propelled herself into my arms and molded her mouth to mine. There was no hesitation, no doubt. It was simple biology. She wanted me.

I didn't care what it was. I welcomed the opportunity of forgiveness with open arms. Spinning her around, I pushed her over the back of the couch, reveling in her scent as I unzipped my jeans. I couldn't think of anything but being inside of my mate. Palming myself in my right hand, I bunched her short skirt in my left and wasn't at all surprised to find that she was bare and ready for my cock underneath.

Wanting to be absolutely certain this was what she wanted, I asked, "Are you sure, Korrina?"

"Fuck me," she demanded. "Now, Oswin."

I obeyed, closing my eyes and sinking deep into her blistering hot heat. With unintelligible words, I growled out my satisfaction. She was impossibly hot, impossibly tight—I couldn't get enough of her. And when she bucked against me, moaning in pleasured pain, I dug my fingers into her hips, roughly dragging her back to me, unable to control my actions. I wasn't in control. The wolf knew he had to be docile before, to let her take the lead. But now? No. There would be no discipline now. He would take her how he wanted. And he wanted her hungry, desperate for him. He wanted her to come to him when she wanted this. He wanted her all to himself. Klive and Obsidian be damned.

Moving my hands to her breasts, I nibbled down her jaw to the mating scar on her shoulder, worrying the spot with sharpened canines before I broke the skin, careful only to taste the sweet blood that flowed freely from the wound.

"Oswin!" she screamed, shuddering and gripping the sofa so hard the wood groaned as she reached her climax.

"I'm sorry, darlin'. I'm sorry," I said guiltily, licking and kissing the healing skin before growling out my own completion.

Both of us breathing heavily, I eased out of her and turned her to face me. She looked wild, untamed, and hungry. Fuck, it made me hard for her all over again.

"Bedroom?" she asked, pushing her long hair back from her face.

Without hesitation, I lifted her into my arms and jogged to the master bedroom. Setting her on her feet next to the bed, I closed my mouth over hers, dipping my tongue inside, careful to avoid her fangs. She groaned as the taste of her blood hit her tongue and pushed me onto my back.

Straddling my hips, she rocked her wet flesh against my cock and purred, "I want to taste you, Oswin," before positioning me at her entrance and sinking down.

I moaned, nodding my head and gripping her hips. It would be so easy to come right now. I had to be in control.

Korrina ran her tongue from my chest to my jugular, nipping and teasing along the way. Every prick from her sharp fangs made me gasp, not in pain but in pleasure—extreme pleasure. I wanted this, wanted her teeth in my neck, my groin, my wrist—wherever she wanted to put them. I wanted to be inside her like she was inside of me.

"Do it," I told her, baring my neck. "Take what you need from me."

For one fleeting moment, she stared at me, unsure. Then, as quickly as her doubt began, it ended. Smiling, she moistened her lips and struck rapidly, burying her fangs into what I offered. There wasn't any pain from the bite, just a sharp sting of pressure that seemed to be connected to my dick every time she pulled a mouthful of blood from the wound. Moaning in ecstasy, she rode me slowly, moving in time with her swallows, until she broke away, threw her head back, and screamed incoherently as she came.

When she was still and silent, I rolled her over, lazily lapping at her mouth before lifting her knees and plunging deep. She hissed in pleasure, her amber eyes flitting open and glowing in the darkened room. Encouraged, I pounded into her faster and harder than I ever had before. In the past, she was fragile, breakable. As a vampire, she wanted everything I could give her and more. Howling, she wrapped her legs around me and let me ram myself home until I yelled out my own release.

***

Hours later, we were still in my bed, but now damp and satisfied from another round in the shower. Korrina was half-sprawled on top of me, running her fingers through my chest hair, while I drew slow, languid circles on the small of her back and savored the satisfaction of having my mate in my arms after a very enjoyable tryst, one that would be repeated as soon as she gave me the go ahead.

"I can feel your smug smile from here," she griped.

"You can't complain when you're the one that put it there," I told her, kissing the top of her head.

"I guess that's fair." She placed an absentminded kiss on my abdomen and gave me a curious look. "Are you going to tell me why you were at the bar today? I find it hard to believe it was a coincidence."

"It wasn't. I was there to talk to you … on your own terms. I don't want to pressure you."

She smiled. "Yeah, that hasn't worked well for you in the past, has it?"

I smacked her bare ass. "Smarty-pants."

"Ow!" she grumbled.

"Oh, stop. I've seen you take a lot more than that and love it." I wriggled my eyebrows at her.

She shook her head. "Uh-uh, nope. We were having a conversation that didn't involve our private parts. Don't get sidetracked."

"Your hand is ten inches away from my very lonely cock," I deadpanned. "I'm doing what I can."

"I think you can do better," she reprimanded, giving said cock a playful slap. "Now, what was it you wanted to talk about?"

I groaned. "Something that is decidedly not sexy."

Her eyebrows rose. "And that is?"

"Your satyr friend."

"Agapios?" When I nodded, she said, "He is not my friend. He's an acquaintance, at best."

"Okay, so do you know why this 'acquaintance' is prowling around the pack-lands?"

She frowned. "No. Has he been back since the last time I spoke to him?"

"Not on the lands, but he's definitely been snooping around the boundaries."

"What do you think he wants?" she asked, sounding worried.

"I think he wants you," I told her, keeping my voice level. "Tell me about him. Would he have a reason to search for you?"

She scrunched up her face in concentration. "Not specifically. He was with me when I was last arrested, but he didn't seem angry about it."

"What punishment did he receive?"

"I have no idea. Like me, it was his third offense, so I'm sure he was banished in some way. Solon would've given us similar punishments. He's all about being fair."

I nodded. "Okay, tell me about satyrs in general. I need to know what we're dealing with."

"Okay, well, the Romans liked to romanticize satyrs as sensual, half-man, half-goat beings that frolicked alongside nymphs in meadows while playing flutes. But in real life, satyrs are cunning, manipulative creatures. While they vary in degrees of beauty, they are all highly sexual and are known for becoming obsessed with possessing something or someone they covet. Oh, and that goat thing was something the Romans invented, too. The Greeks' mythological version is much closer. I've never seen one with an actual tail, but the horse-like ears and erect phallus thing? That's dead on."

I furrowed my brows. "Would he want to possess you?"

"It's possible, I guess, though he never has before, and we've known each other since we were younglings."

"Can he hurt you?"

"Not really, but he can hurt the ones I love. Satyrs hypnotize people. They plant false memories. Sometimes, they even make their victims do things they wouldn't ever do, like kill someone … or kill themselves."

"I think we need to talk to Solon," I told her, holding her close. "And maybe, turn on the electricity in the boundary fences."

She looked alarmed but nodded. "I think you may be right."

# MAKING A MAN OUT OF A CAT
## KORRINA

"I have to go out of town for six weeks on Thursday," Klive told me. He was leaning over my shoulder, reading the search results I was perusing on his laptop.

"Oh, yeah?" I asked absentmindedly, not paying much attention to him. I was desperate for information on Agapios' address and/or whereabouts.

Oswin and I had been trying Solon and Obsidian on their cells for two days and still hadn't heard anything back from either of them. I had passed the worried stage thirty-six hours before and was now hurdling into a crazy 'let's call the FBI, the Bureau, and maybe, a SWAT team' territory.

Klive hopped over the back of the couch and laid down next to me. "You're not listening … again. Give up the search for a while and watch a movie with me." He batted his long golden lashes at me. "Pretty please? I think you need to take your mind off this for a little while."

I closed the laptop with a heavy sigh. He was right. I wasn't having any luck with the search, anyway. "What kind of movie are we talking?"

"I was thinking something with Clint Eastwood or something set in World War II."

In horror, I reopened the laptop. "No, thanks."

Laughing, he reached across me and closed it again. "I'm kidding. We'll compromise, okay?"

"By compromise, do you, by chance, mean that you'll watch what I want and hate it the whole time?"

"That is exactly what I mean," he told me, his blue eyes twinkling the afternoon sunlight.

"Fine," I said, yawning as I nestled my back into his chest. "Where's the remote?"

"Same place I put it when you made me watch six episodes of Pride and Prejudice. You know, Korrina, not everyone has the same appreciation for Colin Firth in the bathtub."

I snickered. "Says you."

"Fine," he said, sounding very put-upon as he sat up. "I'll get the remote, but a rom-com is as far as I go."

"The Holiday?" I asked hopefully.

"Okay, but only because there's a sex scene in there."

"You would know, perv."

He dumped me into the floor as he got up. "I have eight sisters, jackass."

"Hey!" I yelled, laughing as I got to my feet. "I totally deserved that."

"You definitely deserved that. And because you've misbehaved, I'm not going to give you some of the cheese popcorn Keona made for me today."

I sat back down on the couch and pouted. "But … cheese."

"You are so adorable when you're petulant," he said, shaking his head as he brought in a bowl of popcorn and the remote.

I preened. "Gorgeous and bearing popcorn … talk about irresistible!"

"That is not true."

"My ass!"

"And a beautiful ass, it is," he said, giving me a peck on my forehead. "But my severe lack of female companionship should tell you just how wrong you are."

"You don't have a severe lack of female companionship. I'm here. And I've been told I have a beautiful ass and that I'm adorable when I petulant. So, there's that."

He handed me the remote. "Just watch this terrible movie and shut up, you."

***

I didn't remember going to sleep, but I woke up in the warmth of Klive's arms with his very hard cock pressed so hard against my center, he was practically inside of me. I groaned as he shifted his hips away, missing the delicious friction already.

"Good, morning," he said.

"Why didn't you wake me?" I asked, chuckling sultrily.

He kissed my temple. "You looked so peaceful. Your face was so untroubled as you slept in my arms."

I smiled and kissed his muscled forearm. "I think that about you when you're sleeping, too."

"I'm not sleeping now," he told me, running his nose along my hairline.

"Are you saying you're troubled?"

"Troubled? Korrina, I'm barely under control. I want to mark you, to fuck you—it's instinct to make you mine." Angling his head, he breathed in the scent of my hair. "Your scent is heavenly. There's an earthy, floral scent under the shampoo, almost reminiscent of the smell of the forest during our monthly run. It's intoxicating. You're intoxicating."

"Thanks." I laughed huskily. "But I kind of knew you felt that way since the first night we met."

He seemed surprised. "You did?"

Smiling deviously, I answered, "Yeah, you were quite the chatty Cathy when you were half-asleep. You told me I smelled good and even called your Alpha a dumbass." I popped my eyes open. "I pretty much love you for saying that, by the way."

131

"I'm not going to lie. My heartbeat doubled when you just said you loved me."

I smiled and tapped my ear. "I know."

He laughed. "Well, since you're omniscient, you probably know that Oswin is a dumbass. What else do you call someone who gave all this up?"

My forehead wrinkled in confusion. "All what?"

"Are you kidding me? You … your smell, the feel of your heat against my cock. You make my animal scratch to get out. He wants you."

My eyes flickered from amber to grass green as my nymph side's interest was piqued. "Do you want me, Klive?"

"We are of one mind," he growled, shuddering as I intentionally grazed my naked flesh against his sizable erection.

"Then I'm glad I'm not wearing panties," I said, shifting so he had better access and a hand on my breast.

His eyes widened. "Are you sure you want this, Korrina? If my palm wasn't overfilled with your breast, I would have thought I misunderstood the 'almost sex' we had the other night at the bar."

"You tell me if I want this," I said. "You're the one with the extraordinary sense of smell."

His eyes went pure gold as he pulled me tighter against him. "The sweet scent of your arousal is maddening."

"Klive, please," I urged, wanting so much to have him inside me finally.

He shook his head as if he was coming out of a lust induced fog. "Fuck. This is really happening, isn't it?" When I nodded, he asked, "Do we need protection?"

I cocked my head to the side, a questioning expression on my face. "From Oswin?"

"From a litter of baby hybrids," he corrected.

"Oh!" I shook with silent laughter. "No, nymphs only get pregnant when they want it to happen. We'd be pregnant all the time, otherwise."

Klive's breath caught when my eyes changed to a brighter shade of green and delicate vines started to grow from the curly tendrils of my hair. I could see the animal stilling within him as he watched my transformation. "You're so fucking beautiful, Korrina," he said in awe. Leaning forward, he pressed into me, breathed me in, and closed his eyes with a sigh. "I love the smell of the forest on your skin."

"I love the feel of your cock," I said, hissing when the move pressed his length even tighter against me. "Please, Klive, don't think about this. Just fuck me."

Groaning, he tightened his grip on my waist. "I want to. Believe me."

I chuckled softly and glanced at his struggling face. "And I want to believe you. I really do. But you're not inside me, so…"

Closing his eyes again, he took another deep breath as if he was trying to work up the courage to tell me a dark, mortifying secret. "Korrina," he said finally. "I've never done this before."

"Done what?" I asked, my voice throaty and hoarse with desire.

He clenched his jaw and hesitated a moment before he answered, "Had sex."

Careful of the rock-hard erection between my legs, I twisted around in his arms. "Are you serious? Never? As in, never ever, never?"

"As in, I'm a virgin. There it is—the ugly, embarrassing truth."

Speechless, I stared at him for a few beats. "How? You're a full-grown male—a very sexy full-grown male."

He scrubbed a hand down his face, no doubt hating he had to tell me this about himself. "I'm a full-grown lion, Korrina, a genetically flawed lion. No female wants someone who isn't normal."

"Normal." I harrumphed. "What's normal? I'm a nymph that got turned into a vampire. Abnormal is all we creatures of the night have. It's the new normal. But this virgin thing, Klive." I bit my lip. "Are you sure there aren't any females in the pack you're interested in for sex?"

His canines grew long as he ran his thumb over the lip I'd bitten. "I can't give them pups, Korrina. I have to mate with someone compatible to have offspring."

My fangs emerged as his thumb stroked my mouth again. "Oh."

He licked his lips. "But, now that you mention it, there is someone in the pack I'm very interested in."

In a soft, breathy voice, I asked, "Then why not let your first time be with her?"

He traced the low neckline of the v-neck dress I wore, stopping close to my taut nipple. "I'm trying to, but you seem reluctant for some reason."

"Very funny," I said wryly, then I frowned. "Klive, are you sure this isn't something you should do with someone you love."

"Are you done trying to get out of this?" He cupped my breast and squeezed lightly. My breath caught, and the fresh scent of my arousal filled the room, making his cock jump in anticipation.

"Klive," I said, my expression serious. "You're a virgin."

"Korrina," he said, equally as serious. "I'm fully aware."

Exasperated, I disentangled myself from him and stood up, pulling off the dress and thin chemise I wore in the process. I stood before him, completely naked, and without a bit of shyness. "Klive, I'll do this. But only because you're kind, and sweet, and

134

really kind of gorgeous, but just so you know, this is not a normal way to lose your virginity."

"Everyone's experience is different," he pointed out, grinning indulgently. "Holy fuck. You're perfect."

"Different," I repeated, weighing the meaning of the word in my head. "Yep, I'd definitely say this is that."

"Korrina, take your own advice," he urged, getting to his feet and smoothing out the furrowed line between my brows with a thumb. "I've never been so terrified in my life, but I'm choosing to trust in your guidance. So, don't overthink it, okay? Please, just fuck me."

I nodded and let him lead me to his bed with an expression of uncertainty peeking through the lusty fanged smile I was giving him. "I just want to make this good for you."

"Same here," he assured me. "I have serious doubts that my beginner skills will match up to anything you're used to with your vampire husband or Oswin. They are both very old, and age equals experience in the supernatural world. I am certain that includes what goes on in the bedroom."

I glanced down to the tent in his boxers. "I think you'll do fine."

Klive prowled closer, his nostrils flaring before he took me down to the bed and kissed me—really kissed me. He kissed me with every bit of the pent-up hunger he had been saving up, his hands moving across my body with purpose—instinct guiding him to all the places that made me moan for more.

And my hands? They were on his cock, silkily stroking him toward orgasm as I writhed against his testing fingers. I was so ready, so wet for him, he didn't have to know what he was doing; my body did that for him. It led him where I wanted him to be.

"Please, Klive," I begged, wanting more, wanting his animal.

Without another second of hesitation, Klive spread my knees apart and drove into me, ignoring the sound of my sudden half-pleasured, half-pained cry. Pulling back slightly, he slammed into me again, his animal rushing to the forefront. I could see it in his burning, golden eyes as he stared down at me.

I met the stare head-on. "Make me come, Klive," I told him. "I want to come while your big cock is buried inside me."

Growling loudly, he began to pound into me in earnest, the thrusts nearly painful in their intensity. "Whatever you want," he hissed in an inhuman voice. "I will give it to you."

Boy, did he ever. I came almost instantly, screaming out his name, my body going rigid with an orgasm so intense my whole body seemed to spasm.

He never slowed for a second. His cat couldn't. He wouldn't. To him, there was no sense in it. This was simple, natural. I was a female, and he was a male. This is what we did.

"I like the way you scream my name," he hissed into my ear, letting his canines trail across my collarbone in two twin lines of pain.

"I like the way you make me scream," I purred. "Your cock is so big ... so hard. It fills me up when you fuck me."

He gasped loudly as animal lust clouded his vision. Alarmed, he pulled out of me and backed away from the bed with a feline move too quick for me to follow in my satiated state.

"Klive?" I panted, lifting to my elbows to look at him. "Are you okay?"

Though I would have never thought he'd be brave enough to do it in front of me, Klive grabbed his dick and stroked it as he looked me over. With my hair wild, my eyes half-lidded, and the scent of my arousal, I knew he had to do something to appease the animal. His lion was wild to get back into me, scratching at the surface to be let out as he fucked me.

"Can't ... control ... him," he bit out, gripping the back of a chair so hard he reduced it to splinters. "You have to get away from me."

"No," I said, sliding off the bed to walk toward him. "You need to come inside of me."

His growl was loud in my ears as he tracked my approach. "You ... don't know ... what you're saying," he said through gritted teeth.

I backed away slowly, capturing the lion's attention. If he wanted to play hard to get, so be it. Two could play that game. "Here kitty, kitty."

Claws emerged from his fingertips, fangs in his mouth. The cat was in control. "You want to play, little female," he asked.

I showed him my own fangs. "You know what I want."

Without warning, he pounced, missing me by a mere inch. He was much faster than he looked.

"Are you even trying to catch me, kitty cat?" I taunted from the living room.

He slinked to the doorway, no doubt willing himself to be gentle when he caught me and found me relaxed on the couch, waiting for him. "Where will you run now, female?" he asked.

"You don't think I can take you?" I asked boldly, easing myself up to prepare to run.

"Oh, you'll take all of me," he promised, corralling me into a corner.

I froze involuntarily when I heard his words, knowing the chase was over.

He smiled like the cat that ate the canary. "Here I come, little kitten."


I woke to the warmth of a strong male curled around my naked body. Nuzzling my face into the crook of Klive's arm, I sighed contentedly as what we'd done this morning replayed in my mind. Feral and wild, he'd been unrelenting as he fucked me, no matter how many times he or I came. Honestly, if he hadn't simply exhausted himself, I was sure he'd still be fucking me now, but instead, he'd collapsed sometime around one o'clock, still hard as steel inside of me.

"I can smell how much you want me," Klive growled huskily into my ear. "It makes me so hard for you."

I shuddered, unable to think of a reply. I wanted him to dominate me, to fuck me until I begged him to stop, and then refuse to like he'd done this morning.

As if he could read my thoughts, he moved on top of me and speared between my legs, plunging deep. "I don't want this to be the last time we do this before you're ready to have my cubs," he said suddenly. "No one has ever wanted me the way you do."

I met his sincere gaze and laid a palm on his tanned cheek, I whispered, "Whenever you want me, I'm yours."

Klive caught my hand as I moved it away and pressed my palm against his lips. The gesture was so romantic, so full of love, I might have swooned if I wasn't already on the carpet. "I'll always want you," he said. "I'll never stop wanting you."

I smiled seductively. "Good."

With a growl of pure want, he lifted my legs around his hips and drove himself to the hilt, pressing my wrists to the floor on either side of my head. My body arched up as his small, measured thrusts became long, hard ones that made me beg for more. Seconds later, I squeezed my eyes shut and screamed out his name as an orgasm shot through my body. A self-satisfied smile was spread across his strikingly handsome face when I opened my eyes. He'd enjoyed watching me orgasm, making me reach my orgasm.

"Is it as good for you as it is for me?" he asked, peppering my neck with kisses.

I chuckled softly. "Klive, I'm pretty sure you have a magical cock. Is that what you wanted to hear?"

"A little bit, yeah," he told me, grinning smugly. "What guy wouldn't want to hear that from the hottest female on the planet?"

"You think I'm the hottest female on the planet?" I asked, shamelessly grinding myself against his cock. I was so wet, so ready for him.

He looked surprised at the question. "Yes. One hundred percent, yes."

"Liar." I thrust my tongue between his lips and dipped into his mouth to taste him. Fuck, he tasted good.

Moaning, he gripped my hips and made quick work of filling me again. I cried out into his mouth but let him take control. With brutal thrusts, he pumped into me, lifting my slight weight up as he forced his cock into me over and over. I bore it beautifully, begging for more and arching my body in ways that heightened the pleasure for both of us, until, suddenly, my whole body seemed to seize up. I collapsed to the floor beneath him, panting heavily from my second orgasm in as many minutes.

Klive smiled down at me. "You're so sexy when you come."

Amber-eyed, I lifted my head and gave him a fanged smile. "You make it so easy."

His cat purred in satisfaction. "Do I?"

I brushed my lips against his and took the opportunity to thrust my tongue past his budding fangs to taste his mouth again. Groaning, he deepened the kiss and began to mimic the rhythm of our tongues with his hips.

"Korrina..." he started, then he stopped, unable to articulate what he needed me to understand.

Somehow, I knew already. Klive wanted me as his mate; there was no one else for him. He wanted me to understand that I was his possession, no matter how many other males were in my life.

With my breath heavy with anticipation, I said, "Do it, Klive," and pulled my long hair to the side.

Eyes full of gratitude, he sank into me the exact moment he made me his mate. I quaked against him, my body rocking with an orgasm so strong, I could feel the tight throbbing throughout my whole body. Growling out his own release, he buried his face into my hair, and I couldn't stop myself from sinking my own fangs into his shoulder. Yelping in pain, exquisite and erotic, he spilled into me, and we collapsed, sated and mated, to the carpet.

# A HOMECOMING OF SORTS
## OBSIDIAN

After I spoke to Korrina, I couldn't concentrate on work. I went to all my scheduled meetings, wined and dined suppliers, and even flirted my way into a very lucrative deal with a new client, but I couldn't get the thought of Korrina with another male out of my mind. Why hadn't she mentioned it when I called? It wasn't like her to keep secrets from me. Could she really love Oswin's second that much?

No. I couldn't think that way. I would go insane. Standing up from the minuscule desk in the tiny Italian hotel room I'd rented, I grabbed my bag to pack. I would have to cancel tonight's drink engagement with a potential client, but that was the least of my concerns. I wasn't going to sit halfway around the world and let another shifter take my wife. She belonged to me.

The pack-lands appeared exactly as they had on my last visit, but there was one thing that was definitely different—there wasn't one bit of animosity in the air. The menacing vibe that had been so prevalent before was gone. It was peaceful, calm, welcoming even. I cut the engine of the rental car when I pulled into Oswin's and went over what I was going to say to Korrina when I saw her. What could I say? At this point, I just wanted her in my bed tonight, and not some other male's.

With determination of steel, I opened my door and stepped out only to be nearly bowled over by the blur that was my wife's paramour. "Fuck, I'm glad you're here," he said, obviously half drunk.

"Where's my wife, Oswin?"

"The cafeteria. I think she's washing dishes."

141

I lifted my brows in surprise. "Korrina's doing dishes?"

"Well, fuck, someone has to."

I put my hand on his shoulder. "Are you okay, old friend?"

He shook his head. "I hardly know anymore."

Leaving the distraught werewolf to his bottle of whiskey, I followed Oswin's directions to the cafeteria and found Korrina elbow deep in suds, her hair scooped up in a haphazard ponytail.

"If that's more dishes, just put them on the counter," she said without turning around.

"I really didn't think I'd find you here," I said, giving her a smacking kiss on the neck.

"You're home!" she screeched, kissing my face everywhere she could reach it. "I thought you'd be gone another week!"

"I missed you too much to stay any longer," I said, kissing the top of her dark head. She smelled of the forest and flowers. There wasn't a hint of wolf to be found. "What are you doing?"

She nodded toward the sink full of dishes and sighed. "Everyone likes to eat, but no one likes to clean."

"The one universal truth that will stand the test of time," I said distractedly, looking at all the prep work yet to be done. "Now tell me why you're really here? Are you stress cleaning?"

"Maybe," she admitted.

"Why?"

"Just your garden variety guilt," she said, turning back to the dishes. "That's all."

"Well, snap out of it."

She started in surprise at the uncustomary curtness in my voice. "Okay, but it might be a teensy bit harder than that."

I crooked my finger. "Get over here, my love. I'm going to make sure you don't have time to worry."

Against her blazing pink flush, her eyes were greener than I'd ever seen them before. "What did you have in mind?" she purred.

Handing her a knife, I said, "Well, I was thinking we'd start with the onions and garlic. You know, get them out of the way. Then we can move on to the less pungent vegetables."

Confused, she furrowed her brow. "Huh?"

I gave her a mischievous smile. "Chopping vegetables wasn't quite what you had in mind?"

She returned my smile, showing me the tips of her fangs. "Not even close."

I stared at her mouth for a moment, at war with myself. After a few of her heartbeats, I said, "Let's go home, Korrina. This can wait a few hours."

"I thought you'd never ask," she said, giving me a peck on the lips. Giddy, she dried her hands, left a note for someone, and then met me at the door.

Dropping a kiss to her brow and cheek, I lingered a long moment before saying, "Tell me about Klive."

The smile on her perfect face fell. "Oswin told you."

"Who else?"

"I'm sorry, I didn't tell you myself," she said, bloody tears pricking in the corners of her eyes.

"Me, too, love. But don't cry. I'm not upset," I lied.

"You aren't mad?"

I answered her question with a question. "Are you going to divorce me and marry Oswin's second?"

Wide-eyed, she shook her head furiously. "No!"

"Then I'll get over it." I tucked her tiny frame under my arm and let her wrap her arms around my waist as I led her to the passenger side of the car. "Will you spend the night with me tonight?" I asked.

She stood on the tips of her toes and pressed her full, pouting lips to mine. "Always, Obsidian. You never have to ask."

The quick trip home was incredibly revealing. The few times I glanced at Korrina proved to be very fruitful. The agony of her choice was apparent even behind her sunny smile. She regretted her actions, regretted straying from me.

A lesser male would have exploited the situation, made her make promises of monogamy and exclusivity. I wasn't that petty. I knew she had other obligations … and an extensive nymph lineage.

But inside our home, with the doors closed behind us, the air between us was stale, unmoving, the atmosphere tense. Neither of us moved beyond the foyer. We knew things had to be resolved before our reunion.

I waited for her to speak, wanting to hear what she had to say for herself.

"Obsidian, I …" she trailed off when I raised a hand to stop her explanation.

"Do you love him?" I asked. I had to know that first.

"Yes," she admitted, her gaze lowering toward the floor in shame.

I closed my eyes and let out a long breath. "Like you love me?"

She shook her head. "Nothing like that. He was alone, sort of an outcast, and still a virgin because he's not a wolf. It did start out as a revenge tactic, but it … uh, progressed to something more."

"So you fucked him out of his loneliness?"

She smiled sweetly, her green eyes twinkling. "Yes?"

I narrowed my eyes at her, and her smile fell away. "If he isn't a wolf, what is he?"

"He's a were-lion." She twisted her wedding ring around her finger nervously. "The Williams family adopted him when he was a child and raised him as a wolf with their eight daughters."

I sighed, not knowing what else to ask or say. I wasn't mad about her fucking Klive. Far from it. He was a virgin, for Pete's sake, and with eight sisters, he probably treated her with a reverence that I could never duplicate. But, that didn't mean I wasn't going to use the situation to my advantage. Korrina was a very compliant lover. Even more so when she was contrite.

"He didn't—"

I put a finger to her lips then impulsively replaced it with my mouth. Just as I knew she would, she tasted as sweet as honey as she moaned into the kiss and clutched the lapels of my jacket in her tiny hands.

Breaking the kiss, I pried her hands from my jacket and pushed her away gently, asserting control. "Go to the bedroom, strip the bed to the fitted sheet, and get undressed," I told her. "I'll be in there in a minute." She left immediately and without a word, unbuttoning her shirt as she quickly ran upstairs. I exhaled a long breath and shook my head in wonder as I watched her walk up the stairs topless. She made me so hard for her. I was kidding myself if I thought I was in control of any situation she was involved in. She would always be the one pulling strings.

That certainly didn't mean I wouldn't try, though. Deciding to toy with her a little, I willed myself into mist and drifted upstairs to hover near her as she took off her skirt and underwear and then ripped the comforter and sheet off the bed in obvious haste. I felt a swell of pride knowing that she was determined to please me even with her other lovers so eager to please her.

It was with a ridiculously gratified ego that I admired my wife's beauty as she stretched out cat-like on the bed. Unable to wait for a second longer. I misted around her body, solidifying just enough to tease her, to caress her, to touch her in the places that made her gasp with pleasure. Her response to my touch, however light, was instantaneous. She bowed up off the bed and cried out my name with genuine want in her voice, in her movements. She was an instrument of pleasure for me to play to the best of my ability, and by God, I would play like the devil himself had possessed me.

Materializing into flesh and bone beside the bed, I ripped off my shirt and unzipped my trousers to release my erection. Korrina watched me, panting through parted lips. My cock throbbed in time with the sound of her breathing. It was like thunder crashing in my ears.

"Come to me," I said. She took my hand with no hesitation, allowing me to position her at eye level to my cock. Hands threaded in her hair, I held her still as I filled her waiting mouth, pumping fast and hard. Ripping the belt out of my pants, I doubled it over, gripping it tightly. Korrina whimpered in anticipation, and the scent of her arousal filled my nostrils. She wanted to be punished.

I jerked myself out of her swollen, wet mouth and trailed the edge of the belt along her bottom lip. "Tell me what you want, beautiful."

"I want you," she said, looking hungrily at my cock.

"Just me? And not this?" I ran the belt down her back and over a rounded cheek. She shuddered and arched up against the leather, offering herself up for any punishment I was willing to give her. "I thought so."

My hand trembled slightly as I stroked my wife's cheek. I stared at it, unsure of what I was seeing. Vampires didn't shake. They also didn't let their emotions control them, yet here I was contemplating locking Korrina in the attic to keep her away from her other lovers.

Shaking off the fog of jealousy, I spun Korrina around and pressed her head into the mattress. Raising my arm high, I brought the belt down just hard enough to make her scream. Over and over, I let her feel what I felt—the betrayal, the hurt, and when my desire to punish her was finally sated, I forced myself into her, smiling when she cried out, first in pain and then in climax.

Limp and tearstained, she collapsed on the bed, breathing heavily. I didn't give her a second to rest. Grabbing a handful of her hair, I forced her head up and hissed, "We're not done here, Korrina." I hissed into her ear. She whimpered, but I knew she would take anything I gave to her and want it as much as I did. "On your stomach, love," I told her. She obeyed instantly in an effort to please me. And please me, she did. Straddling her, I felt like a king as I rubbed my cock against her from behind, testing her wetness. "Is this what you want, nymph?"

"Please," she begged. "Fuck me, Obsidian. Please."

More than mollified by her wanton desire, I pushed the tip of my dick into her, barely moving. "Is this want to want?" I asked again.

"Please," she cried out, needing more.

Irrationally irritated, I grabbed the belt from the bed and held it in front of her face. "Bite down on this."

She eagerly complied, taking the leather between her teeth seconds before I thrust forward, filling her as I slipped my hands underneath her to palm her breasts. She cried out, almost dropping the leather from her clenched teeth when I cruelly pinched her nipples. "If you drop that belt, I will use it on your ass again," I growled. "And this time, I won't be nice about it." She nodded, tears running down her cheeks. Leaving one nipple pinched between my fingers, I slipped my other hand between her thighs and moved two fingers slowly over her swollen clit. "Do you want to feel me come inside you, Korrina," I asked. She nodded fiercely, moaning behind the leather strap. "Good, girl," I told her, moving my hand from her breast to her hair. Tugging her hair back, I made her look at me as I hammered into her hard and without mercy. Screaming behind the belt, she tightened around me, reaching her crescendo just as I came, spilling deep inside of her.

With gentle hands, I pulled her sweaty hair from her face and took the belt from her mouth. She sighed and let her head fall forward, exhausted. I kissed the back of her neck and smiled against her skin when she shivered. "Want to shower with me, Kore?"

She laughed weakly. "The water spray is really going to hurt."

# EVERY DOG HAS ITS DAY
## KORRINA

Alone together in our home, something felt off with Obsidian. He wasn't being himself. Though we'd had sex (albeit strange, unusually rough sex) before, he seemed reluctant to speak to me, to look at me now. What I'd thought would be a very promising homecoming, was turning out to be the opposite. It was cold, distant, not at all what I'd expected.

I was tempted to ask him what was wrong with him, but I was almost positive I already knew—Agapios had gotten to him. Asking him would reveal nothing. A satyr's victim never remembers that they've been spelled into doing his bidding. They only remember after the task is complete … if they survive.

Acting as though I was oblivious to the control Agapios had on my husband, I watched him cross the room, pick up a book, and settle into a chair. That's when I made my move. On my hands and knees, I crawled to him, letting my hair trail behind me in curly tendrils of flowering vines. Yes, I was laying on the charm … big time, but I had to be sure. Obsidian could never resist me in this form. Add the fangs, and he was even more of a goner.

Lowering the book, he watched me approach him with interest. "Come here, Korrina."

I crawled between his knees, praying I'd been wrong to think he'd been brainwashed.

He smiled cruelly, taking my jaw in his hand. "I want you to put that sinful mouth to use, Kore. I've always loved the way you suck my cock."

I didn't hesitate to unzip his pants and take out his long, smooth length. As scary as it was for me to obey him, I yearned to do this. My nymph side craved it. His touch, his smell, it was all I'd known for the past three years; I could never deny him.

As I enveloped him in my mouth, he groaned and gripped my hair in his hands to force me into his preferred rhythm. "Look at me," he growled. "I want you to know whose cock is in that talented little mouth of yours."

I lifted my eyes to his and nearly jerked away. His eyes were black, completely black.

Obsidian laughed. "Not who you were expecting?" he asked. "Is it an animal you want? Perhaps, a wolf or a lion? Do you like it a little rougher now? Is that how they give it to you?"

He didn't give me a chance to answer. Yanking me up by my hair, he pulled me off my knees as he stood and slung me face first into the chair he'd been sitting in.

"Is this how they fuck you, Korrina? Do they take you like a beast?"

My cry was muffled by the cushion as he ripped my panties off and drove into me.

"Answer me!" he yelled, jerking my head back as he thrust into me as deep as he could.

"Yes!" I sobbed.

"You whore!" he thundered. "I leave for a week, and you just can't help yourself! Who else did you fuck while I was gone?"

I screamed as he twisted my hair in his hand.

"Answer me!"

"No one!" I shrieked. "I swear!"

His breath was harsh in my ear. "Liar. I smell Luke Rivette. I can smell his scent right now."

"I don't know why his scent is here! Obsidian, I didn't fuck him!"

"No, she didn't."

With a roar, Obsidian pulled out of me and stood to face our neighbor. In all the commotion, he didn't hear Luke come into the house. "Get out, mutt!"

The wolf didn't move. "Mr. Raines, I want you to step away from Korrina. Right now."

"Why? Do you want to take my place?" He scoffed, walking toward the stairs. "Go ahead. I'm fucking done with her."

"Mrs. Raines, are you okay?" he asked, grabbing me gently by the arms to set me upright. His face was calm, but I could see the alarm in his eyes.

"Luke, I…" I trailed off, not able to get the words out through my sobbing hiccups.

He cast an angry look up the stairs, then put his arm around me to lead me out the front door. "I'm your friend," he said, handing me a clean purple bandanna for my face. "You can tell me anything."

"Obsidian is possessed," I told him, wiping my eyes. "Luke, I'm sure of it. This isn't him."

His eyebrows raised as he turned toward the house. He looked ready to smack some sense into Obsidian, vampire landlord or not. "It sure looked like him."

I stopped him with a hand on his arm. "No, this reeks of satyr magic."

"Satyr?" he asked, his forehead furrowing. "Those exist?"

"Yes, and I have a history with this one. His name is Agapios. We lived in the same town. I think he's been lurking around the pack-lands for almost a week, ever since the night of the meeting."

Luke tensed and pulled me closer. "Come on, I'll drive you to Oswin's. You can tell me what he's done to Obsidian on the way."

"Okay," I said in a small voice, willing my lips not to tremble as I spoke.

Taking a deep breath, he scented the air. "Let's go," he barked, leading me in a brisk pace as we crashed through the brush. Within three minutes, we were standing on his porch. "Will you come in? I think I may have some clothes that will fit you."

"Sure," I said, more than happy to accompany him. I didn't want to wait outside alone. Even with the trees and their constant vigilance, I was terrified to be so exposed.

"Come on, then," Luke said, giving me the 'ladies first' motion.

I walked into the foyer and started. The room was exactly as I had left it. Not one single thing had been changed. "Uh, Luke?" I asked, laughing through my tears. "I see you've done absolutely nothing with the place."

He shrugged and looked around the room. "It reminded me so much of where I lived with my Abigail, I just couldn't. She loved those old whitewashed walls and antiques. Painting the walls would've felt like an insult to her memory."

As I listened to Luke speak tenderly about his mate, my heart broke for him. What must it be like to have to live without your other half? How could he even function? I walked to the mantle and picked up a framed picture of a cute brunette with bright blue eyes. "Is this her?"

He shook his head. "That's April, my sister. She lives in Baton Rouge with my parents."

"She's pretty," I told him, setting the frame down and moving on to the next picture. When I stopped, I gasped. This female I knew. "Luke, why do you have a picture of Kia on your mantle?"

"That's Abigail," he whispered, gingerly taking the picture from my hands. "This was taken right after we met."

"She looks—"

"Just like her," he said grimly. "I know."

"This is why you don't live on the pack-lands?" I guessed.

Luke let out a weary sigh. "I can't. I just can't be around her." He looked skyward and sighed again. "Even their voices are exactly the same, Korrina. I'm not going to lie; when I heard Kia say my name for the first time, I nearly wept in front of her."

I squeezed his shoulder. "That's completely understandable."

He put the frame back on the mantle and seemed to shake off whatever thoughts were plaguing his mind. "Look, the fact of the matter is, I don't want to burden Kia with my grief, and I don't want to torture myself. It's better this way. Way better."

I didn't believe that for a second, but I kept my mouth shut. That was a long, long conversation for another day. Right now, we had to see Oswin and find Solon. We had a satyr to catch. That was the only way to take the spell off Obsidian before it was too late.

"I'm nearly ready," I told him pulling off my nightie and pulling on the long t-shirt he gave me without a bit of modesty.

He shielded his eyes and turned around quickly. "Good. Let's go."

*** 

Once Luke and I were on the road, I started telling him about Agapios, what he could do, who he was to me, and what had to be done to restore Obsidian. He took everything in stride, offered to help, and even offered to track him in the woods, but I didn't want to make any decisions without my mate. There was only so much I could handle on my own.

"So, I guess I should tell you before I drop you off, Oswin has had a few tonight."

"A few what?"

"Beers, shots of whiskey, various other alcoholic concoctions. He was kind of having a bad day."

"Why? What happened?"

He gave me an impish grin. "You happened, sweetie. He heard you giving Klive the ride of his life last night, and when Obsidian

153

came home, he heard you with him. It was sort of a double whammy. He did not take it well."

I frowned, too embarrassed to be indignant at his humorous take on the situation. "What am I walking in on here?"

He pulled behind Oswin's truck and put the transmission into park. "Oswin is a male who adores his mate. Nothing more, nothing less. Now get on up there and knock. I'll wait here until he lets you in."

I kissed his cheek. "Thanks, Luke. I mean it."

He blushed but played it off. "Hey, what are friends for?"

"Fast getaways?" I asked, giving him a grateful grin before hopping out of the tow truck. Waving, I ran to Oswin's porch and rang the doorbell three times in quick succession, waiting nervously as I scanned the quiet street for movement. Everything looked the same. Nothing seemed amiss, but I knew that didn't mean a damn thing. Agapios was a master at hiding, lying in wait, and getting what he wants. How else could he convince a two-time public indecency arrestee, like me, to fuck him behind the Starbucks half a decade ago?

I'd almost given up on Oswin being sober enough to answer the door when he opened it, stumbled forward, and tugged me in by my belt loops. "Hey, darlin'," he said, smiling a sleepy, goofy smile.

I gave a 'thumbs up' to Luke, who blew his horn as he pulled out, and closed the door behind me, catching a whiff of whiskey in the air. Oswin was in no shape to take care of a satyr problem at the moment. "Are you okay?" I asked him.

He staggered forward, trapping me against the door in between his strong, steely arms. "Fuck, Korrina. You're just so fucking … you." He ran his knuckles over my cheek and breathed me in, eyes closed. "I dreamed of this face, this scent, more than I ever dreamed of fucking you. It was your face I'd see when I went to bed, when I woke up, when I touched myself to try to alleviate the insatiable hunger my wolf felt for his mate, that I felt for you. I couldn't tell you before, but fuck it, I can now. I love you, Korrina. It's not the beast and the bond. It's the man inside of me. He would die for you."

Unblinking, I could only stare at him for a few moments. "I don't think that will be necessary." I laid my palms on his deliciously muscled bare chest. "You know, it's very late. Shouldn't you be sleeping by now?"

He gestured to his pajama bottoms and bare feet. "I was, but a seductive female woke me up and made me answer the door."

I slid my hands up around his neck and leaned in close, a natural reaction to his obvious flirtation. "Maybe that seductive female had a good reason for waking you up?"

Blond eyebrows rose above citrine eyes. "Really?"

"Not that good of a reason," I amended, knowing he wouldn't be able to deal with a lunatic Obsidian right now.

"But you'll come to bed with me, won't you?"

Grinning at the exaggerated expression of angst as he waited on my answer, I shook my head and said, "Sure. Lead the way."

I didn't know it before, but ten seconds later, I learned that 'lead the way' translates to 'pick your mate up and carry her bride-style to the foot of the bed before dumping her face first onto a particularly rough wool blanket' in werewolf. "Ow," I said, laughing into the blanket before righting myself.

Oswin climbed onto the bed next to me and stretched out in a big X. "I'm sorry, darlin'. I seem to be lacking finesse this evening."

"I hope you're not insinuating that you're suave or anything … because you're not."

Smiling with his eyes closed, he said, "You have to, at least, give me moderately charming."

I pursed my lips. "Yeah … no. Not in a billion years. How much have you had to drink tonight?"

He sighed. "The whole village is talking about it, you know—the younglings under the stars or whatever."

Rolling my eyes at the lightning fast speed of the pack's grapevine, I asked, "Are you talking about the younglings that are possibly decades away?"

"I know, it's just, it's one thing when you're with Obsidian; he's your husband. But Klive? Korrina, that eats me up. The first time I heard you two … together, I wanted to kill him, to strangle the life out of his eyes, but then he … uh, did something … I don't know. It…" He trailed off as if reluctant to tell me.

"Something?" I prompted, climbing over his leg to curl up next to him.

"He did something that made you make this sound you make when you're with me," he said finally, his gaze so intensely blue-green, I couldn't look away. "It turned me on, Korrina, when really, it should have horrified me." He sighed. "Baby, I don't know which one is more fucked up—me having to hear you with Klive or me wanting to hear you with Klive."

I fought hard not to show the shock I felt, feigning nonchalance for his sake. I wanted him to feel like he could talk to me about anything … even this. "So," I said. "You thought alcohol would help you decide?"

Oswin flashed a grin. "It's never led me too astray."

Pursing my lips disapprovingly, I shook my head. "Why don't I believe you?"

He growled out a low chuckle. "Because I'm a known liar."

My eyebrows shot up. "I think you should drink more often. I kind of like it."

"Do you think I wouldn't admit that when I'm sober?" he asked.

"No, I know you wouldn't. There's no way in hell, Oswin. You're a secretive bastard.

"Well, while I'm in the sharing mood, can I tell you something else?"

"Of course. Lay it on me."

He smirked at my choice of words. "Don't think I won't."

"Don't think I'll stop you," I retorted, daring him with my eyes.

Turning on his side, he propped himself up on his elbow. "I fucking hate that you've mated Klive."

My heart seemed to skip a beat when those words sunk in. No, I realized. It wasn't the words—it was the underlying danger in those words. His tone was calm, light, but the edge of animal in his voice made the hair on the back of my neck stand up.

"Would it be better if it were someone else?" I asked.

"It would be better if you were only mated to me and fucking Obsidian."

I kept silent, waiting to see where he was going with this.

"You see; your husband feels like he's taking the high road with all of this. He thinks you should be given a break because you're a nymph. But that's horse shit, and you know it, Korrina."

What could I say? He was right … sort of.

"Oswin, a few days ago, I would've agreed with you. I did name Klive as my consort in retaliation. But there's something between him and me—a connection of sorts. It's not the kind of love we have. It's more like our spirits recognize each other because of what happens in the future if that makes any sense. Does that make any sense?"

He rolled to his back and sighed. "Yeah, I guess it does. I fucking hate it, but yeah. I'd like you to explain what you meant when you said that it wasn't the kind of love we have, though."

Shrugging my free shoulder, I said, "What he and I have is innocent; it's pure. You and me, we're decidedly not innocent."

"Do you still love me?" he asked, holding his breath.

I rolled my eyes. "Of course, I love you, Oswin. I'm your mate."

He barked out a cruel little laugh. "My mate … sure."

Sitting up, he turned to me. I followed suit. He had his serious face on.

"All right, Korrina, if you love me so much, why were you going to take Klive as a lover before we even had a chance to reconcile?"

I traced the blanket's stitching with my finger, trying to work up the nerve to say what I had felt.

"Tell me what you're thinking, darlin'," he pressured.

"You hurt me," I said softly. "Really hurt me. I loved you. You have no idea how much. Hell, I don't think I knew how much until the moment I found your hiding place in the great oak blown to smithereens. I couldn't breathe, Oswin, thinking that I'd lost you. And then you dumped me. You ran away."

He didn't let me say another word. His lips met mine before I could utter another syllable. Leaning into the kiss, I moaned my satisfaction into his mouth. It felt so good to feel him wrap his arms around me and know exactly how he felt—to know that I had mattered more than the petty grievances he had against Obsidian. It was just nice to know that he really loved me.

Breaking the kiss, I laughed and said, "You taste like whiskey."

"Is that good or bad?"

"Good," I said, pushing him back onto the bed so I could nuzzle into his scruffy neck. I missed this—the closeness. Oh, all right, I just missed him, the stupid werewolf.

"Korrina?"

"Hmm?"

"Will you forgive me for denying those annulments requests now that you understand?"

I smiled against his skin. "Yes."

"You're a good mate to me," he said, yawning and closing his eyes. "I don't deserve you."

I looked up at Oswin's sleeping face when his grip loosened and thought that it was funny that he'd chosen the words he did because I was just thinking the same thing about myself.

*** 

After Oswin went to sleep, I showered, changed into the clothes Oswin bought for me, and started searching the internet again, trying any and every conceivable combination of Agapios' name, residence, and hobbies. I couldn't find anything. Finally, in desperation, I went to Facebook and typed satyr into the search bar. Agapios' face stared back at me. Yelling with triumph, I glanced over to see if Oswin was still sleeping then clicked on the page. Nothing. Not one single bit of personal information, only check-in at The Cheetah Lounge, which I was pretty sure was a strip club. Choking back a sob, I felt a hand close over my arm.

"Darlin', what's wrong?" Oswin asked, opening his arms and gesturing for me to curl up with him.

As always, I took a split second to appreciate how fiercely handsome Oswin was. Though his brow was furrowed with worry, his blue eyes were sharp and focused on me with a protective intensity that made me weak at the knees. He exuded strength and safety with his every breath. I knew that if anyone on this planet could help me, it would be him.

"Agapios has Obsidian!" I wailed, bursting into hysterical tears.

Alarmed, he grabbed me by my upper arms and shook me a little. "Where, Korrina?" Without waiting for an answer, he rushed to his feet, shed his pajama pants, and grabbed a pair of jeans from the closet. "Where does he have him?" he asked again, yanking his jeans up and pulling the first t-shirt he found off its hanger.

"It's not like that," I said miserably. "He's possessed him, turned him against me."

He paused his manic dressing. "What? How?"

"I think he ran into him while he was on a layover in Atlanta."

His brow furrowed. "What makes you think that?"

"He was fine when I last spoke to him. He was excited to see me, to be home. Something had to have happened somewhere in between there and here. And I know Agapios has been in Atlanta. Here, I'll show you. Where's your phone? Mine is almost dead."

Oswin pointed out his phone on the nightstand and sat beside me on the bed to watch as I typed. As soon as the page loaded, I felt him go still. "That's Ambrose Lucas. He's a new client of Oswin Enterprises."

"Ambrose Lucas?" I gave him an "Are you an idiot?" look and shook my head. "Oswin, that loosely translates to Immortal from Lucania. That's Agapios' hometown." Suddenly wary of his nearness, I asked, "You haven't met him in person yet, have you?"

He kissed my forehead. "No, darlin'. We only spoke on FaceTime. I'm one hundred percent myself."

"Good." I sighed. "This can't be a coincidence. It just can't be."

"No, I don't think it is," he said, lost in thought, his face serious again. "If Solon still hasn't answered. I think it's time we go to him. I'm starting to worry that Agapios might have gotten to him, too."

I froze. That thought had never even crossed my mind. "Oswin, we need to go. Now."

"Let me get my boots on. If we leave now, we can be there by dusk."

"What will you tell Klive?"

"Nothing. Let him go out of town. He's safe there, and he'll be none the wiser."

I zipped up my jacket and headed for the door. "Oswin?"

"Yeah, darlin'?"

"Are we going to be okay? Obsidian hurt me last night. I'm a little scared."

He strode to me and wrapped me in his arms. "I meant what I said to you last night. I would die for you."

I hugged him tight and buried my face his massive chest. "Let's just pray it doesn't come to that."

# HELPING YOUR MATE'S HUSBAND 101
## OSWIN

The closer we got to Meadowbrook, the more wracked with anxiety Korrina became. She hadn't voiced it, but it wasn't hard to tell with the way she was gnawing on her bottom lip like it owed her money. I couldn't blame her. Though Obsidian wasn't in any immediate danger, that could change in an instant.

"Any chance Solon will still be at his office?" I asked, mere seconds from turning onto the streetlamp lined entryway to her hometown.

"It's possible, but I doubt it."

"Good. That driveway with the wisteria really freaks me out." I glanced over and grabbed her hand. She was as white as a sheet. "Are you okay?"

"I'm fine." She gave me a distracted smile and watched as lights flickered on in the houses as we passed them.

She was uncomfortable to be here. That much was obvious, and if you asked me, she had darn good reasons for it. For one, her parents still hadn't forgiven her for letting me threaten them on the day of our mating, and for another, vampire blood was the drug of choice for nymphs. If the bedroom lights lighting up around us were any indication, it wouldn't be long until they started to harass her to be charitable. That wasn't going to happen. Not with my mate.

"It's the first right, the second house on the right," Korrina said, pointing toward a sign that read Bottlebrush Lane.

I turned down the wide street and parked in Solon's darkened driveway. "Think he's home?"

"There are no lights on. His car is gone, too. I don't think he's here."

Disappointed, I asked, "Where would he be this time of night?"

Korrina gave me a knowing look, accompanied by a wriggling eyebrow. "He is a nymph."

I laughed. "I have a hard time imaging straight-laced Solon Manetas making a booty call."

"Well, imagine it."

Shuddering, I said, "I'll pass. What now?"

She looked sharply to the right when several lights lit up the yard next door. "Let's check into a motel for a few hours. If anyone here knows where Solon is, they'll tell him we came by. The Raven's Nest Inn is about two miles away."

I glanced left at more lights blazing to life. "Is that far enough?"

"I really hope so," she said, her face tense.

That made two of us. Backing out, we left the subdivision and drove to the small motel on the outskirts of town and checked in. It was small, and its cleanliness was somewhat of a subjective thing, but it was safe and away from prying eyes.

Once in the room, Korrina sat on the bed like her feet wouldn't hold her up anymore. "Why is he doing this to me?" she asked. "This can't be just because he blames me for our arrest. He's an asshole, not stupid."

I put the duffel bag I'd brought on the table and sat next to her. Resting my chin on the top of her head, I sighed and said, "Because, darlin', unlike me, he doesn't have a way to hold on to you. I can't believe I have to tell you this, but you are tough to resist. You leave such a lasting impact on every soul you meet. Whether it's with your beauty or with your genuine heart, you touch everyone."

She glared at me with somber green eyes. "So, you're saying this is my fault?"

"Yes. That's exactly what I'm telling you," I deadpanned, rolling my eyes. "You know that's not what I'm saying, little nymph."

"Can your little nymph sleep in your bed for a while?" she asked, a small frown line creasing her smooth forehead. "I'm scared."

I raised my brow. "Of whom? Agapios?"

"Yes, and Obsidian. You don't know what he was like."

"That wasn't him," I told her, but I knew that wouldn't stop her from her constant worrying. I held her close, stroking her cheek with my thumb. "We'll figure out what we need to do when Solon deigns us important enough to call back. I promise, darlin'; we'll fix this."

Her face crumpled as if she was remembering a particularly painful memory. "I'm glad you're here with me," she said, burying her face into my neck.

"I'd do anything to keep you safe, Korrina," I whispered. "Anything."

Fresh tears sprung to her eyes. "I love you, Oswin."

My heart pounded in my chest. I would never tire of hearing her say those words to me. "I brought you something to sleep in, on the off chance you'd need it," I said, kissing the worried furrow between her brows. "I thought you might not want to sleep in your jeans."

She gave me a wry look. "That's really thoughtful, Oswin, and really sweet, but I have to ask, is it going to be see-through or leather?"

An enigmatic smile spread across my face. "You'll see."

She shook her head, stifling a yawn. "Let's see it."

Unzipping the duffel, I rooted around for the short spaghetti-strapped gown of some unknown silky material. It wasn't exactly footie pajamas, but Klive's sisters said they thought she'd like it, and who was I to argue with the ladies about sleepwear? If I had my preference, she'd be wearing nothing but a well-satisfied smile while she was in bed with me.

She shot a skeptical look at me when I gave her the nightie. "You picked this out?"

"I never said that," I said, aiming a cheeky grin at her. "I only said I brought it." I crooked a finger at her. "Come here, sugar."

She didn't question it, just came to me and let me lift her shirt over her head and unhook her bra. "Thanks," she said. "I honestly don't think I would've had the strength to do that myself."

"Anytime," I told her, grinning winsomely. "Seriously, anytime."

She rolled her eyes and yawned again before slipping off her jeans and pulling the gown over her head. "Are you coming?" she asked, climbing onto the bed.

I tamped down the urge to say something sarcastic and nodded. "Right behind you ... in the non-sexual sense." Korrina groaned, but I could see the smile she hid in the pillow. "I love you, darlin'."

"Love you, too, weirdo."

***

Korrina slept for almost three hours after I tucked her into the, thankfully, clean sheets and blankets. I watched her the entire time, never taking my eyes off her peaceful face. I couldn't get over how wrong I'd been about her. In my panic after her death, I'd been so sure she'd end up cold and calculating like Obsidian had been before he married Edith. Now I was angry at myself for wasting all this time and not having any faith that she'd be the same tenderhearted nymph she'd always been.

"You're staring at me again," she complained, sitting up.

I ran my hand up her arm, putting a fallen strap back into place. "Hard not to," I said unapologetically. "Solon texted about an hour ago. When you're ready, we'll go see him."

Throwing the covers aside, she bounded out of bed. "Why didn't you wake me?"

I grinned as I got a peek at her black lace panties. "You were tired. One hour wasn't going to make a difference. Besides, he had … uh, things to take care of first."

"Things?"

"I'll let him tell you about it," I told her and left it at that. She would find out soon enough.

Korrina was fully dressed and back in the truck in two minutes flat, a testament to how badly she wanted to help her husband. As much as I hated the show of loyalty towards Obsidian, I approved of her protectiveness. It showed exactly how fierce she could be in order to shield the ones she cared about from harm's way. That was one thing I could relate to on many, many levels.

Five minutes later, we pulled into Solon's drive. He was waiting for us there, worry plain on this face. "What's happened?" he asked us as soon as we stepped out of the car.

"Can we come inside?" I asked. His neighbor's lights were popping on one by one, flooding the darkened street with light. It wouldn't be long until we had an audience.

"Of course," he said quickly. "Come on in."

Once inside, Korrina burst into tears. "Solon, Agapios has been stalking me, and he's done something to Obsidian."

Hugging her close, Solon said, "Whoa, now. Let's not have any of that. We'll figure this out." He looked at me and lifted an eyebrow.

"We need to know where Agapios is, Judge Manetas. And we need to know how to take his hex off of Obsidian. The sooner, the better."

Solon nodded and went to his library. He came back carrying a file as big as a phonebook. My eyes widened. What kind of deviant were we dealing with?

"All right," Solon said, opening the file. "Let's see what we have here." He perused the papers, while Korrina paced the floor, chewing on her fingernail.

When she walked past me for the tenth time, I finally snapped and pulled her into my lap to keep her still. "Calm down, darlin'. Solon will figure out where he is."

"I see you two have made up," Solon observed as he closed the file.

"Yeah, she couldn't stay away from me," I said, wincing when Korrina smacked me on the arm. "See, she can't keep her hands off of me."

Korrina rolled her eyes at our laughter. "What did you find, Uncle Solon?"

"Well, he's supposed to be under house arrest in Georgia for eleven more months, but if you've seen him around the pack-lands, he's found a way to trick the system."

"Let me guess. Is he supposed to be in Atlanta?"

Solon looked surprised. "Yes, how did you know?"

"Obsidian had a layover at ATL. It's the only chance he would've had to put a spell on him."

"Shit," Solon muttered. "Look, I know the procedure is to call the Bureau. Hell, I wrote that law, but you can't do that. Those idiots will get killed or get you or Obsidian killed." He ripped half a page out of the folder and handed it to me. "If you get caught, I'll tell them you stole this, so don't get caught."

I nodded. "We don't plan on it."

"We?" he asked. "Are you planning on taking my favorite niece into certain danger?"

I smiled down at my mate. "Respectfully, sir. I don't think I could stop her."

"No," he mused. "And neither can Agapios, though I bet he thinks he can now that she's a vampire."

"What do you mean?" I asked.

"Satyrs have very little control over nymphs, but other supernaturals are not as resilient to their charm. That's why you're going to wear this apotropaic amulet." He pulled a knotted leather necklace with an eye-shaped pendant out of his pocket. "It will keep him from getting into your head. It might also help Obsidian come out of this trance if you get close enough to him.

I breathed a sigh of relief. "Thanks, Solon."

He smiled grimly before getting up to show us to the door. "Good luck, you two. You're certainly going to need it."

Korrina hugged him and kissed his cheek. "I love you, Solon."

"Love you, too, baby girl. Call me when this is over. I'm getting too old for this."

She shook her head. "You stopped aging at twenty-eight, just like me, Solon."

He shoved her out the door. "Just go before I chain you up in the basement to keep you safe."

I laughed. "Now there's a good idea."

Korrina started walking to the truck, middle fingers both skyward. Solon chuckled. "I guess we know where she stands on the imprisonment idea."

# MEETING WITH THE ENEMY
## KORRINA

Oswin and I made it to the Atlanta city limits in a little under two hours. Five minutes after that, we were parked directly in front of Agapios' apartment building. "Okay, what's the plan?" I asked, trying to mentally prepare myself for a fight I had no idea how to win.

"I thought you had one," Oswin said, a cheeky grin on his face.

Growling in frustration, I smacked him on the arm. "Oswin! This is so not the time for you to be yourself!"

He gingerly rubbed his arm. "Damn, Korrina. I need this arm to kick the satyr's ass."

"Sorry," I said, in a distinctly unapologetic voice. "My tolerance for danger-related humor is very low when my husband is the one in danger."

"Duly noted," he said, his face becoming serious as he studied the apartment building in front of us. "See that pecan tree by the balcony?"

I leaned over his way and nodded. "Yeah, he goes by Fred."

He turned back to me, a look of confusion on his face. "What?"

"That's what he says his name is," I told him, shrugging my shoulders.

Oswin shook his head, amused by this. "Well, Fred has a great view of this entire block. He might know where Agapios lives. Can you do me a favor and ask him if he's seen a satyr?"

I gaped at him. "This is exactly why I wanted you involved. You have a great head for wargames."

He laughed. "When you're an Alpha male, wargames are all you've got. If you ever spend more than a couple days with me at a time, I'll tell you why that is, darlin'."

I smiled. "I'd really like that." Impulsively, I added, "I love you, Oswin."

He reached across the seat and pulled me closer to nuzzle his face into my hair. "And I love you, Korrina. I plan on showing you exactly how much as soon as we take care of our little satyr problem."

Lust shot through my body, hot and wild, as his rough beard scratched my cheek. "I'd like that, too. A lot."

"All right, back to the problem at hand, before we have another sexual encounter of the truck variety." Oswin adjusted himself and grinned at me when he caught me watching. "What does our friend, Fred, have to say about our little problem?"

I closed my eyes and blocked out everything but the pecan tree. Concentrating hard, I sent my questions to him and waited for a response, which was almost instantaneous in its arrival. Hot tears sprang to my eyes as soon as they popped open. "He says that Agapios lives in 3-B and that Obsidian is there with him right now."

"Fuck!" Oswin shouted, hitting the steering wheel.

I stared at him, wide-eyed. "What is it?"

"Nothing," he muttered. "It just complicates things, sugar. I didn't want you involved, but now it's two against one. The plan has got to change."

Steeling myself, I sat up straight. "What do I need to do?"

"You're going to go up and knock on Agapios' front door, while I break into the sliding glass door on his balcony. Ask Fred which one is 3-B."

I pointed almost straight ahead at the third floor. "That one."

He grimaced. "Of course, it is."

"What's wrong?"

"I'm not a huge fan of heights. Will you ask Fred if it's okay if I use him as a ladder?"

Fred jumped at the chance to be a part of the action when I relayed the message. He thought this was the coolest thing that had ever happened to him. "He's definitely on board," I told Oswin.

"Good." He slipped a hand behind my head and kissed me hard. "Don't get out of the truck until I'm at up there, okay?"

I nodded, trembling a little. "Got it."

He opened the door. "See you soon, darlin'."

I panicked, grabbing his jacket sleeve. "Oswin!"

Alarmed, he closed the door and cupped my face in his hands. "What is it, baby doll?"

My mind whirling, I could only get out, "Just be careful, okay? Promise me, Oswin. Please."

"I knew you really loved me," he said, grinning before pressing his mouth to mine again. "I never gave up hope."

Crossing my arms over my chest, I said, "I don't hear a promise in there."

He laughed and kissed the tip of my nose. "I promise, Korrina."

"Thank you," I said, breathing a huge sigh of relief. I didn't know why, but just hearing him say the words made me more confident about our 'fly by the seat of our pants' plan.

\*\*\*

In the time it took me to shake off my fear and prepare to exit the truck, Oswin had sprinted across the lawn, climbed up Fred like Spiderman, and motioned for me to go.

Scared, like I'd never been before, I took a deep breath and got out of the truck, walking briskly to the stairs and sending up a prayer that this wouldn't turn out to be the stupidest thing we'd ever done.

Just as I expected, Agapios knew I was at his door before I could even knock. The satyr's talent to scent out another creature almost rivaled my vampire ability. "What do we have here?" he asked, snatching the door open and giving me a knowing smile.

I sighed and tried to keep my eyes from rolling back in my head. I had no patience for his bullshit today. "Agapios, I know Obsidian is in there. The trees told me. Let me see him, or I'm kicking your ass from here back to Meadowbrook."

"Brave words, little vampire," he said, tsking me like a small child caught with their hand in the cookie jar.

Clenching my teeth together, I growled. "I'm fucking serious, Agapios. Send him out here. Now."

"How about you come in here?" he offered.

"Fine," I said, storming past him. I found Obsidian immediately. He was sitting on the couch, eyes blank and hands resting in his lap. He looked like a robot waiting to do his programmers bidding. I turned on Agapios. "What have you done to him?

"Me? I barely lifted a finger. You did most of the work. Well, knowing you, I doubt you'd consider it work."

"What are you babbling about, Agapios?"

"Just that the trance he's under is of your own making. All I did was make sure that it was there. You kissing him three times is what set it into stone."

"And might I ask why you're doing this?"

"Why?" he asked angrily. "Why?" He grabbed a handful of my hair and painfully brought me to eye level with him. "Because my dear, you fucked me out of my life. Because of you not being able to control that sweet pussy of yours, I got banished to this fucking hellhole, while you, your uncle's favorite, got to go live on your own, surrounded by males who wanted you. I have nothing here, no females to fuck, nothing to do but watch these stinking humans doing their boring day to day. You fucking owe me, Korrina."

He shoved me away, and I fell to the floor, wincing at the pain in my scalp. "You're fucking nuts."

He darted to where I sat on the floor and kicked at me, catching me in the stomach. "What did you say to me, whore?"

"Whore?" Growling, I leaped up and charged him. We both crashed to the ground, punching and scratching at anything we could reach.

Mere seconds after our tussle started, Oswin burst through the glass door, snarling like a rabid pit bull as he snatched Agapios off of me and punched him so hard, he went flying over the couch.

"You all right, darlin'," Oswin asked, helping me up while keeping a watchful eye on Agapios and Obsidian's whereabouts.

"Fine," I wheezed, holding my stomach.

He frowned as Agapios moaned and tried to get up. "Excuse me for a minute."

"Sure, why not?" I asked, collapsing onto a low stool next to the front door.

In a blur of movement that was almost too fast to see even with my vampire sight, Obsidian came to life, stopping Oswin's stalk toward his prone master with an arm. At first, I thought he'd just punched him in the chest to wind him, then I saw the blood and the silver handle of the blade sticking out of his chest.

"No!" I screamed, running into the fray to get to my mate. He couldn't die. Not Oswin. Not like this.

Before I could crouch down to protect my mate from further attack, Obsidian swung around, caught me by the face, and shoved me backward over the couch. I landed on my back next to Agapios with a bone-rattling thud. Shaking off the dizziness in my head, I tried to get to my feet only to have Agapios drag me up by my throat. He laughed at my weakened struggles and ripped open my shirt, exposing my breasts.

"I couldn't make you do what I wanted with you when you were a nymph, but I can do it now, can't I?" He pressed his erection into my stomach, and I moaned in pain, clutching his body closer in instinct. My feet wouldn't hold my weight. "You and I are going to have so much fun," he continued, smiling a nasty grin. "But first…" He looked over his shoulder at the vampire awaiting instructions. "Obsidian, take the knife out of the Alpha and cut out your heart. I'm going to fuck your wife while she watches the two of you die." He turned his grin on me. "Two down, one to go."

I watched Obsidian as his expression went from panicked, to defiant, to resolved. He had tried to fight the command and had failed. Bending, he jerked the knife from Oswin's chest, the pain making the wolf grunt and drop something he held tightly in his grip.

"No!" I screamed, making Obsidian notice me for the first time since my arrival. His face went thunderous, seeing me pinned against the wall by Agapios. I pleaded with my eyes for him to do something, anything, to end this.

"Do it!" Agapios snarled back at Obsidian, not even bothering to take his greedy eyes from me. He was so sure his power over the vampire would prevail, he missed the blink of Obsidian's eyes, the shake of his head.

But I didn't miss it. With a small nod, I accepted the blade Obsidian handed me in silence. I knew he wasn't quite himself yet, but, at least, we had more of a fighting chance. We could win this.

"What's taking so fucking long," Agapios yelled, finally turning to find out why his sycophant hadn't obeyed him yet.

Obsidian bared his fangs in a vicious snarl. "Take your fucking hands off my wife," he demanded, a loud growl erupting from his chest.

"Sit down, vampire, and shut up," Agapios said, laughing when Obsidian shrugged and did as he asked.

"Hey, Agapios," I said weakly, bringing his attention back to me.

"What?" he spat.

"You forgot about something."

"What's that?" he asked, ripping my shirt all the way open and pinching a nipple cruelly between his fingers.

I smiled through the discomfort, fangs extended. "You forgot that I'm a vampire."

Agapios' eyes went wide a split-second before I lunged at his neck and bit hard into his jugular. He screamed wetly, pushing me away with his waning strength, but I held on, watching the blood bubble out of the wound, thick and fast, to stain the white linoleum floor beneath us.

With his life force fading, he fell to his knees, and I followed him down, unable to hold myself upright. "What? You don't want to fuck me now?" I taunted.

His words were garbled, but I distinctly saw him mouth, "Fuck you, whore."

I raised the silver handled knife above his chest and laughed at the fear in his eyes. "Agapios, how would you like to become a vampire?" I asked.

His eyes widened. "Noooo…" he gurgled.

"Are you sure," I asked, glancing over to Obsidian who was tending to Oswin. "I think having me as your sire would be a fitting punishment for your misdeeds. You could fetch things for me, feed my husband when he needs blood, and even cook for the wolves in my pack. I think you'd enjoy that, Agapios." I chuckled. "And don't worry, I'll let you stick your cock in a female every century or so. Unlike you, I'm not completely heartless."

Blood pouring from his neck, Agapios whimpered and struggled to get away from my maniacal raving. With a roar, I yanked his face back to mine and held the knife up. I was too far gone to pity his sad state, too angry at what his treachery had cost me. I wanted him to feel the fear I'd felt while I watched the life fade from his terrified brown eyes. He deserved that fear. He deserved it and so much more.

"Korrina," Obsidian called gently. "Come here, my love."

With Agapios' last breath taken, I dropped the knife and crawled to Oswin's side, my heart tearing in two as I felt our mating bond disappear. "Is he…"

"Yes," Obsidian said sadly. "He is."

# THE MAKING OF A NEW BREED
## OBSIDIAN
### *THREE MONTHS LATER*

"Where do you want the ice chest?

Obsidian?" Klive asked, lugging a heavy bright red cooler out of the back of his truck.

"Around back, if you would," I told him. "Need some help?"

"Naw, I got it. I could use someone to help me drink all the beer in here, though."

"That, I would be glad to help with. I need something to wash down the twelve casseroles the ladies dropped off this evening."

"I can help with the casseroles and the beer," Luke said, coming around the house from the backyard. He was wearing an apron that said *I Like Pig Butts And I Cannot Lie* and smelled like hickory smoke. "Come on back, Klive. I'll show you the secret to my rib sauce."

Klive looked hopeful. "Seriously? That's like the holy grail of barbecue sauces."

"Yep, sure is," he said. "Consider yourself one of the luckiest weres in town." Luke winked at me as he followed Klive and his ice chest to the backyard.

I smiled back at him and mouthed, "Thanks."

It wasn't that I didn't like the young lion; I did. More than I wanted to. Hell, it was nearly impossible not to. But sharing my wife with another male, no matter how much of a nice guy, was always going to be a stretch for me.

"Brace yourself," Korrina called, coming out of the woods between the pack-lands and our house. "Incoming casserole!"

"Are you shitting me?" I asked, dumbfounded by the sheer amount of baking that was going on over there. "Is there a casserole dish left on the shelf at Walmart or are they all on my dining room table?"

"They're all on your table," Oswin answered, coming out behind her. "Just wait. The potato salad is on its way."

I groaned. "Southern females and their food ... it's never-ending!"

Oswin laughed, his bright white fangs fully extended. "They're just appreciative, Obsidian. You saved their Alpha's life."

"I realize that, but it's been three months," I complained. "And they know I can't eat all of this."

"No, but luckily, you have a wife who can eat her weight in casserole and potato salad." He patted the slightly rounded belly that held our young and winced when she smacked the back of his head.

"You're all fucking dead to me," Korrina seethed. "As soon as I pop these younglings out, I'm kicking all of your asses for doing this!"

"Promises, promises," Oswin said.

I gave him a small shake of my head. "Don't push it, Oswin. The morning sickness phase hasn't completely run its course."

He nodded. "Ah, sorry, darlin'."

"Not as sorry as you're going to be," she muttered.

"Korrina! I thought I heard your dulcet tones," Luke said, jogging around the house to kiss her cheek. "I sure hope you intend on cleaning up that potty mouth before the babies get here."

She huffed. "Don't count on it."

He put an arm around her shoulders and led her toward the backyard. "Come on, grouchy. I've got ribs with your name on them."

She threw her arms around him and squeezed. "No one understands me like you do, Luke."

"I know," he said good-naturedly. "It's my curse."

Chuckling, Oswin handed me a bottle of blood and grabbed one for himself as we watched an amused Luke lead my wife and his mate away. "Life is good. Eh, Obsidian?"

I clinked the neck of my bottle to his. "Brother, it's more than I could have ever hoped for."

*To be continued with Too Cute To Spook coming Early Summer 2019!*

## Books by J.D. Nelson

### Wicked Ways Series

*A Night of Wickedness*
*All I Want For Christmas Are My Two Front Fangs: A Wicked Ways Companion Novel*
*Wolves Will Be Wolves*
*Too Cute To Spook: A Wicked Ways Companion Novel*

### Night Aberrations Series

*Night Aberrations*
*The Fire within the Night*

### Tales of Desire

*Control*

### Havenwood Falls Sin & Silk Novellas

*Plans Laid Bare*
*Soul Laid Bare*

## About the Author

JD Nelson is a Bestselling Author of Fantasy Romance and Adult Paranormal Romance. An avid time-waster, JD enjoys watching TV and listening to audiobooks when she really should be writing. JD loves to hear from her readers. You can contact her through her website, AuthorJDNelson.com, or on Facebook, where she spends an alarming amount of time chatting with her many Author and reader friends, much to the dismay of her continually neglected manuscripts.

**JD Nelson's Facebook**
www.facebook.com/NightAberrations
**JD Nelson's Twitter**
https://twitter.com/authorjdnelson
**JD Nelson's Facebook Fan Page**
www.facebook.com/JDNelsonsNightAberrations
**JD Nelson's Fan Club**
http://www.facebook.com/groups/269730583130725/

ngramcontent.com/pod-product-compliance
g Source LLC
sburg PA
221180626
00007B/2910